Three-times Golden Heart® finalist **Tina Beckett** learned to pack her suitcases almost before she learned to read. Born to a military family, she has lived in the United States, Puerto Rico, Portugal and Brazil. In addition to travelling Tina loves to cuddle with her pug, Alex, spend time with her family, and hit the trails on her horse. Learn more about Tina from her website, or 'friend' her on Facebook.

Also by Tina Beckett

Winning Back His Doctor Bride
A Daddy for Her Daughter
The Nurse's Christmas Gift
Rafael's One-Night Bombshell

Hot Brazilian Docs! miniseries

To Play with Fire
The Dangers of Dating Dr Carvalho
The Doctor's Forbidden Temptation
From Passion to Pregnancy

Discover more at millsandboon.co.uk.

THE DOCTORS' BABY MIRACLE

TINA BECKETT

MILLS & BOON

Published in Great Britain 2018
by Mills & Boon, an imprint of HarperCollins*Publishers*
1 London Bridge Street, London, SE1 9GF

© 2018 Tina Beckett

ISBN: 978-0-263-07564-9

MIX
Paper from
responsible sources
FSC® C007454

This book is produced from independently certified FSC™ paper
to ensure responsible forest management.
For more information visit www.harpercollins.co.uk/green.

Printed and bound in Great Britain
by CPI Group (UK) Ltd, Croydon, CR0 4YY

To my kids.
You make me laugh and support me no matter what.
I love you!

PROLOGUE

Two years ago

TUCKER STEVENSON WALKED out of the clinic a new man.

Only he didn't feel new. He felt old and cynical and very, very tired. But at least he'd severed himself from his past, in more ways than one. What was that old Grimm's fairy tale he'd read as a child? *Seven at One Blow?* Well, he hadn't struck down seven, but two was enough: a vasectomy and a divorce. It did seem kind of ironic that his test for "swimmers" should be scheduled for the very same day his divorce became final.

He'd never in his worst nightmares suspected he and Kady would end this way. Theirs had been the stuff dreams were made of. Or so he'd thought. Yet here he was, making sure what had happened to them would never happen again.

He glanced back at the clinic before pulling his sunglasses off his head and dropping them onto his nose, dimming the view around him as he made his way to the subway station.

It was done. There was no going back.

His doctor, while arguing against the procedure, saying Tucker was too young to make that kind of decision, had finally acquiesced and given him the old snip-snip eight weeks ago. He would not make another woman pregnant, or cause her to go through the horrors and heartache he and Kady had lived through. She'd tried to talk him out of it, saying they were through if he went through with it. But it hadn't changed his mind.

It hadn't changed hers either. Four years of marriage gone, in the blink of an eye.

He bumped shoulders with someone with a muttered apology as he stepped into the crowded station. On his way back to the hospital, a twelve-hour shift stared him in the face. But at least work kept him from thinking. And the change in venue from Atlanta to New York had meant a fresh start, even if it hadn't dulled the heartache of the past. Bracing his feet apart and wrapping his fingers around the grab bar over his head, he closed his eyes and let the steady *whooshing* of the metro keep the painful memories at bay.

If only they'd known when they'd met, things might have been different.

No, they wouldn't. Because while the pregnancy—a year into their relationship—had come as a shock, the tearful yearning in Kady's eyes as she'd shown him the pregnancy test had won Tucker over. She'd desperately wanted that child. Had wanted him to be happy about it. And in the end he had been. A hurried elopement and whirlwind honeymoon had been just like the rest of their relationship, full of explosive passion that left him breathless. It had been that way the moment they'd laid eyes on each other. The rest was history.

"No regrets," she'd said, lifting her glass of sparkling cider and clinking it against his with a laugh. And when Grace had been born... Magic. Pure magic. The perfect world they'd created had seemed complete. Their love unbreakable.

And yet look at them now.

He opened his eyes and hardened his heart. This solved nothing and only put him in a bad place. His patients needed him. And he needed them.

So that's what he would focus on, and leave all the other stuff behind.

At least until he hit his bed tonight and fell into an exhausted sleep.

The subway lurched to a stop, the doors peeled apart, and Tucker joined the throng of people vying for the exit. Seconds later he was headed up the escalator where a shaft of sunlight beckoned, promising a brighter day.

And, with a little luck, a less painful future.

CHAPTER ONE

Present day

KADY MCPHERSON STUFFED the letter from the IVF clinic into her purse as she stepped out of the taxi onto the sidewalk of the conference center. She paused and took a deep decisive breath. As much as she hated being late, nothing could blot her happiness. She was finally going to take charge of her life after all this time.

One glance at her watch had her racing up the concrete steps. She was supposed to have been here five minutes ago. But who knew that getting a cab would be so hard? At least she wasn't the first speaker. But she still had to somehow slide onto that stage without disrupting the symposium.

She showed her badge to the official manning the registration desk. He pointed her toward the second door on the left, where a large cardboard placard was set on an easel: *Managing High-Risk Pregnancies and Deliveries.*

High-risk.

Her tummy squelched just a bit. As much as she loved her job, there were moments like this, when seeing it spelled out in crisp emotionless text sent her mind spinning into the past. As did each case that didn't go the way she hoped it would. She'd spent nights staring at the ceiling in her bedroom, trying to make sense of it all. Which inevitably led to trying to draw her own baby's face into sharp focus. Instead, the image had blurred with time.

Pregnant women were her passion. And she was committed to doing everything in her power to make each one's delivery process as safe as possible. Was it because of the pain she'd gone through when she'd lost her child? Maybe. All she knew was that she was driven to help every woman she could. And every baby.

So here she was in New York, substituting for a panelist at the plea from a sister hospital. She'd come straight from the airport to the huge Westcott Hotel complex—her home for the next week. Hopefully the rest of her stay would be less chaotic than today had been.

She avoided looking at the sign again, instead tugging the heavy door and peering inside. The sound of chattering voices had her sagging with relief. People were still milling around the huge room, looking for empty seats, while someone passed out bottles of water to the panel members on the dais. Evidently she wasn't the only one running late.

Making sure that envelope wasn't sticking out, she shifted her purse higher onto her shoulder and made her way up four steps to the top of the platform.

So far so good. No one had noticed her entry.

She edged past the first three panelists as she tried

to figure out where she was supposed to sit. The crisply folded nameplates were facing the audience, so she had no idea who anyone was. There were still two empty seats up here. Which one was hers?

She reached the first empty chair and leaned over it, tipping the paper name card so she could see it. Someone named Abe Williams. Okay, it wasn't this one.

The person sitting to the left turned slightly to look up—did a second take.

Shock and horror snaked up her spine just as the lights from the huge overhead chandeliers faded and came back up. A signal that they were getting ready to start.

A signal she ignored, her tummy muscles spasming in protest. She pressed a hand to it, gritting her teeth to keep the sudden slash of pain from exiting her throat.

She couldn't think, couldn't speak…couldn't *move*. *Oh, God.*

All of a sudden, Grace's face swam before her eyes in focus once again. Because she was the spitting image of this man, mirrored in those familiar features—that sharp nose, high cheekbones, those blue-gray eyes.

Saliva pooled in her mouth. A quick swallow sent it rushing to join the acidic lagoon growing inside her.

The lights winked again.

"Hello, Kady. Small world." The low, graveled tone that had once driven her wild with need was now tight. With anger? Hatred?

If so, it wasn't reflected in his eyes. They didn't flicker away, just held hers with an impassivity that made her want to cry. The same impassivity he'd shown at the end of their marriage.

It had been two years since their divorce…three years since their daughter's death.

Hurt made her draw a shaky breath, unsure what to do or say. The lights came back up a third time, and the moderator moved behind the podium. He gave them a pointed glance that sent her hurrying down the row without a word. She felt Tucker's gaze follow her.

It could be worse. She could be sitting right next to him.

Worse?

What could be worse than attending the same convention as a man who'd had a vasectomy just to make sure he never fathered another child with you?

She'd pleaded with him. Had begged him to reconsider.

Remembered humiliation quickened her steps.

Never again. She would never rely on another man for her happiness. This time around she would be one in charge of her future. Of whether she had another child or not.

She dropped into the padded metal seat and scooted it under the table, cringing as the legs made an awful squealing sound against the polished wooden floor. The man at the podium glanced her way again, a frown on his face. She mouthed, "Sorry," then dug into her attaché for the notes she'd brought. How was she going to speak when it came her turn?

The crowded room would have been nerve-racking enough, but to have someone who'd once known the most intimate details of her life sit there and weigh her every word?

Her thumb scrubbed over the spot on her finger. Empty, but not forgotten. Neither had her muscle memory erased the habit of reaching for it whenever she was nervous.

Or missing him.

No, she didn't miss him. Not anymore.

The moderator gave a quick summary of the topic and then started down the line of presenters, reading from a sheet that evidently contained each person's professional bio. She stared at her notes, willing the words to make sense. Willing herself to drown out the well-modulated voice from seconds earlier. Her thumb searched for that missing ring yet again.

Stop it, Kady.

She should have been counting people, so she could brace herself for the mention of her ex's name, but since she didn't remember how many seats there were, all she could do was sit there in dread.

"Dr. Tucker Stevenson, pediatric surgeon specializing in fetal surgery at Wilson-Ross Memorial Hospital, New York City."

Her heart twisted. Even the best surgeon in the world couldn't have prevented what had happened three years ago. And Tucker was one of the best.

The moderator moved on to the next panelist, listing dry facts that barely scratched the surface of what made each person live and breathe…and grieve.

"Dr. Kadeline McPherson, maternal-fetal medicine, at Wilson-Ross Memorial Hospital, Atlanta, Georgia."

No mention of anyone's personal life, how many children, spouse's name. Thank God. And she was even more thankful that she'd gone back to her maiden name. Kadeline Stevenson might have caused awkward questions that she'd rather not answer. She suspected Tucker would prefer that little tidbit to remain buried as well.

She gulped.

Buried.

She hated that word. Avoided using it like the plague.

Speech. Read your speech.

Fiddling with her thin sheaf of papers that contained words she'd recited hundreds of times, she prayed for a clear head. The question-and-answer phase was the trickier part, trying to think up responses on the fly.

With Tucker sitting in the same room.

Forget about him, Kady.

The table microphone inched its way down the line as each person finished.

Tucker's turn came, and his voice cut through her all over again. So much for forgetting about him.

His words were sure and firm, with a confidence that came with being the top in his field.

Kady closed her eyes and tried to drown him out with a bawdy mental rendition of "Ninety-nine Bottles of Beer on the Wall", but it didn't work. Especially since he'd sung that very song to her during her labor to take her mind off the pain.

If only she'd known the real pain would come months after the baby's actual birth.

"Fetal surgical intervention is necessary in any number of cases. My most recent involved an obstructed urethra in an eight-month-old fetus. Surgery removed the blockage and mother and baby were both fine."

They were both fine. How many times did he say that in a day?

Light applause followed his speech, just like it had everyone else's. Kady realized she was the only one not clapping, but just as she went to join in, the sound died away, leaving her with her hands up, palms facing each other.

Tucker chose that very moment to glance her way. One side of his mouth quirked up, a crease coming to life in his right cheek.

Her breath caught as a spark of something dark arrowed through her abdomen. For a few awful seconds she couldn't look away. He evidently didn't have the same problem, giving his attention to the next speaker, who talked about controlling blood pressure in patients with preeclampsia.

She wasn't making that mistake again.

She focused on some nameless audience member as the microphone moved again, capturing the topic of twin-to-twin transfusion syndrome. So far no one had mentioned genetic abnormalities, but no symposium of high-risk pregnancies would be complete without that element. Normally she could just sit there stoically, an expression of polite interest superglued to her face.

But with Tucker sitting just down the row? Almost impossible.

Was he thinking the same thing?

Doubtful. He'd somehow seemed to be able to push Grace out of his life and thoughts with the same ease that he'd signed those divorce papers. Out of sight. Out of mind. Was that how it worked with him?

No, she'd seen his grief firsthand. Raw and angry and ready to wreak havoc on the gods for what had happened. In the end, the only true havoc he'd wreaked had been on their relationship when he'd stated they were having no more children. Ever. She'd had no say. Her request to him to go with her to genetic counseling had fallen on deaf ears. Nothing had moved him from his stance.

And yet a second ago he'd tossed her a smile that had napalmed her senses as if nothing had ever happened between them. As if they were old friends.

They were not friends.

The drone of voices went silent. Glancing up in a panic, she realized it was because it was her turn to speak. The microphone was already in front of her. How had she missed that?

Clearing her throat and hearing it amplified through the whole auditorium made her wince. As did the light laughter that accompanied it. "Sorry. It was a long flight."

More laughter. Louder this time. Maybe because the flight from Atlanta to New York only took a little over two hours.

The emotional distance, though, was much, much longer.

She forced an amused crinkle to her nose. "Long day at the office?"

This time the laughter was with her rather than aimed at her. It helped put her at ease and allowed her to temporarily block out all thoughts of Tucker Stevenson. Plunging into her brief five-minute speech, she allowed passion for the subject at hand to propel her through to the end. Wasn't her specialty all about empowering women during difficult times?

And wasn't that what her IVF quest was all about?

The audience clapped, and she couldn't stop herself from sneaking a glance back down the line of presenters. Tucker was leaning forward, his elbows planted on the table, head swiveled in her direction. This time he gave her a nod that she could swear contained at least a hint of admiration.

For her?

A shiver went through her.

No, she had to be mistaken.

A thought came to mind. Had he gone through with the procedure?

The thought of her ex-husband never fathering another sweet baby girl like their Grace pierced straight through her. He'd been a wonderful daddy—once he'd got over his initial fears of inadequacy. He'd loved their daughter in a way that had made her go all gooey inside—had made her hot for him and him alone. No other man could touch what she'd once felt for Tucker.

Watching as that pristine white casket was slowly lowered into the ground had changed him, though.

It had changed both of them.

Gone had been the days of frantic lovemaking. Of being unable to wait to get each other's clothes off. In fact, Tucker had moved into another bedroom soon afterward, cutting himself off from her completely.

The difference between them was that Kady had never completely let go of hope. Even in the aftermath of Grace's death.

It took two recessive genes coming together to cause Tay-Sachs. He could have had children with someone else and not had a problem. Although since neither of them were of Ashkenazi Jewish heritage, it had never dawned on them that they could be carriers until it was too late. What were the chances?

Enough to land them with a horrific diagnosis.

Any future children they'd produced would have had a one in four chance of having the same deadly genetic imprint.

But there were other ways to have kids. Adoption. Even genetic selection of embryos, although that thought made her stomach swish sideways.

The last panelist finished and not one of them had spoken about genetic abnormalities, which she found odd. Unless there was a dedicated workshop just focusing on screening. She would have to look at the schedule and avoid any such session like the plague.

The moderator opened the floor to questions—the moment she'd been dreading the most.

The first one came from a female audience member and was directed at Tucker. "How many fetal surgeries have you done? And what are the most common things you've corrected? The last question goes along with that. Have you ever had a case that you knew was hopeless?"

The long seconds of silence that followed the query would have made any librarian proud. Only Kady knew exactly what had caused it. And why.

A thousand pins pricked the backs of her eyelids and she had to steel herself not to let them take hold. Instead, she clasped her hands tightly together and willed him the strength to get through the question.

"I've done a few hundred surgeries, although I don't have an exact number. The most common procedures I've run into have been neural tube defects. And, no, I've never had a case where I've given up without at least exploring every available option."

That answer jerked her head sideways to stare down the line at him. He most certainly had. The fact that he could sit there and let that answer fall from his lips made the pendulum swing from sympathy back toward anger.

Only this time he didn't look her way, so her mad face was useless.

Two questions later, someone asked Kady what her toughest case had been.

"That would be my divorce." She laughed as if it was all a big joke, even though that barb had been sent straight toward the hunk to her left. "Sorry. No, my toughest case was a mother who came in at six months carrying quadruplets. She'd had no prenatal care and was seizing—in full eclampsia." A whisper of gasps went through the audience. Kady waited for it to die down, knowing the worst was yet to come. That case had made her cry, and had almost, *almost* made her quit medicine completely. But they needed to know the realities of what they would face.

She forced herself to continue. "Only one of those babies survived. That was hard. I can't stress enough the need for early intervention and care, and you should stress it to your patients as well. Knowledge really is power in cases like this one. If she'd been followed from her first trimester, we probably could have given her a good outcome that ended with four live births."

Even as she said it, she knew—from experience— there were some conditions that no amount of care or intervention could fix.

An hour later, the questions had been exhausted and people filtered from the room, leaving her to stuff her papers back into her bag and plan her escape. The moderator handed her a note. She glanced at it and frowned. The head of maternal-fetal surgery at Wilson-Ross wanted her to stop by his office when she had a chance.

Why? Unless it had something to do with the conference. She made a mental note to swing by the hospital as she dropped the slip of paper into her purse. Her fingers brushed across the IVF clinic's letter, and she couldn't stop herself from glancing at it. It was a huge decision. But maybe it was the best one for her.

"I didn't realize you were going to be here." Someone settled into the vacated chair next to her.

She snatched her attention from the letter, jerking the edges of her handbag closed.

Get real, Kady. It's nothing to be embarrassed about.

"I could say the same thing about you." She hadn't meant that to come out as surly as it had.

His glance traveled from her face to her hand, making her realize her fingers were still clenched around the opening to her bag.

"The difference is," he said, "I work here."

"I was a last-minute substitution. Your administrator asked me to come."

"Ah, so you're taking Dr. Blacke's place, then. I'd wondered who they got."

"Is he traveling?"

"No. He found out he has pancreatic cancer last week."

Up came her head, her eyes finding his. "Oh. I'm so sorry, Tucker. I had no idea. Does he have a good prognosis?"

"Unfortunately no, although all of us have seen hopeless cases turn around completely."

"And sometimes they don't." She forced her fingers to release their death grip on her purse, afraid he'd read some kind of telling emotion into the act.

Ha! As if there wasn't.

"You're right. Sometimes they don't." He studied her for a few seconds before continuing, "Our divorce was the toughest thing you've ever handled?"

"It was an icebreaker. It was supposed to be funny." Especially since they both knew the correct and not-funny-at-all answer would have been Grace's death. "None of them know we were ever married, much less divorced."

"And yet we've been both." His mouth tightened slightly. "Maiden name?"

"Easier, don't you think?" If he could do short, concise questions, so could she. Especially as her heart was beginning to set up a slow thudding in her chest that spelled danger. She needed to get out of there.

"Easier? Possibly."

Possibly? That drew her up short. How did that even make sense? Of course it was easier.

"I think it is. People won't automatically see the last names and wonder if we're brother and sister. Or something else."

One side of that mouth quirked again. "Oh, it was definitely something else."

The thudding became a triplet of beats. Then another. How was it that he could still turn her knees to jelly with the single turn of phrase?

"Tucker…" She allowed a warning note to enter her voice.

He leaned back in his chair. "So how are you?"

"Fine."

Sure she was. Right now, she was anything but fine. Why had she let herself be talked into this stupid trip?

He leaned forward. "Okay, let's cut to the chase. Are you staying for the entire conference?"

"Yes. You?" It was a stupid question, since he lived here, but her brain was currently operating in a fog.

"Hmm…"

She would take that as a yes.

"Do you have a place to stay?" he asked.

A weird squeaking sound came from her throat that she disguised as a laugh. "I take it that wasn't an invitation."

He smiled the first real smile she'd seen since she'd been there. "I take it you wouldn't accept, if it was."

"That probably wouldn't be wise." Not that they hadn't done some very unwise things over the course of their relationship. "The hospital booked me a room at the hotel across the street. It's convenient. And close to both the hospital and the conference center."

"Convenient. That's one word for it."

Was he saying that her being here was making it awkward for him? Of course it was. Just like being around him was uncomfortable for her. In more ways than one.

She took a deep breath and asked a real question. "How are you, Tucker…really?"

"I'm busy." His smile faded, the words taking on an edge that made her tilt her head. And it didn't answer her question.

"You always were in high demand."

"With some people. Not so much with others."

Was he talking about their marriage? Because she hadn't been the one to withdraw. He had. She'd loved this man. Deeply. Passionately. It was why it had devastated her when he'd shut down completely during Grace's illness—pulling away from everyone except for his patients.

She'd been his wife! Grace's slow downward spiral had been just as painful for her. The worst thing was, she'd felt frighteningly alone during those first few months after her death, while Tucker had slept in the guest bedroom and spent longer and longer hours working at the hospital. Desperate to reconnect with him on whatever level she could, she'd casually said maybe they should try to have another baby. If she'd thought that would lure him back into their bedroom, she couldn't have been more wrong. He'd looked at her as if she'd taken leave of her senses, his next words chilling her to the bone.

I'll never have another child.

When she'd started to say something more, he'd cut her off with a shake of his head and walked out of the room. Any time she'd brought up the subject after that, begging him to talk to her, she'd been met with the same stony response. Rather…no response. And his hours at the office had increased so that he'd barely been home at all.

Then had come the final blow. On the first anniversary of Grace's death, he'd announced he'd decided to get a vasectomy, as if it was something people did every day. He'd probably hoped that would end all talk of having more children. It had.

His unilateral decision had floored her. And infuriated her.

The powerlessness she'd felt had been crushing. All-encompassing.

That had been the beginning of the end. Actually, it had been more like a rapid slide to home base, only to find out that the ball had arrived long before you had.

Three strikes and they were out. Bags packed. Papers filed. Divorce decree signed.

Being bitter solved nothing, though. So she stuffed all that back inside.

She went back to his cryptic comment about being in demand. "I'm sure your patients appreciate all you do."

A softness came back into his eyes. "I wasn't trying to be the big bad wolf back then, Kady."

"I can see that…now."

Back then, though, things hadn't been so clear, and he'd seemed like the villain in their particular tale.

To her, anyway. Even now the memory of those days pinched at her heart like a pair of surgical clamps, causing a strange numbness to come over her.

But not so numb that it staunched the weird waterworks sensation that was inching its way back onto her radar. God, she wished things could have been different between them. They hadn't been, though. So she needed to stop looking at him with glasses that magnified those old hurts. "That's all in the past, where I think it should probably stay."

He stood. "You're right. It is. I just wanted to stop by and say hello."

"I'm glad you did. It was really good to see you again."

Good and sad and filled with all kinds of regrets.

He walked away, leaving her on her own once again. Only this time she was ready. All decisions about whether or not to have children would be made by her. And as soon as she got home, she was going to act on them. Seeing him again had just brought home all her reasons for wanting a child, and that longing she'd had as she'd carried Grace over those nine months.

All she needed to do was select a sperm donor and she'd be ready to start a family of her own.

For a few brief seconds she'd wanted to throw that letter from the clinic in his face, the way he'd thrown his decision about not having children in hers, but what would it solve?

Nothing.

She didn't want to hurt Tucker. She just wanted a baby. Not to replace Grace. That would never happen. She would always love her little girl and be grateful for the time they'd had together. At times, Grace's loss still caused her lungs to seize in the middle of the night as she lay there alone in bed. Any tiny sound in the dark would make her sit up, sure she'd heard a familiar cry. Wishing with all her might that she *had* heard that cry. And when she realized no one was there, Kady would be the one who cried.

Surely her daughter wouldn't have wanted her to be stuck in limbo like this, never moving forward. She'd like to think Grace would have wanted her to go on living, to love and be loved. And she was finally ready to share that love. With another baby.

She tried to focus on that and block out the negative thoughts that were steadily creeping into her head.

And the best way to hold those at bay was to stay as far away from Dr. Tucker Stevenson as possible.

CHAPTER TWO

TUCKER HAD NO idea why Phil Harold, the department head, wanted to see him. He was already running behind on his appointments and had a surgery scheduled at two o'clock this afternoon. At this rate, he'd be late to the convention workshop today. The convention. Great. Where he'd probably see Kady again.

How in the hell had any of this happened? He'd come to New York to get away from her. No, not from her. From the pain and memories of what had happened in Atlanta. Except some things—unlike his old golf clubs—weren't as easy to leave behind. Some of them had followed him. And seeing Kady again had been like a punch to the gut, reawaking the guilt of not being able to give her what she'd wanted.

It was just for a week, though. Surely he could maintain some kind of poker face for that long. Then she'd fly back home. Life would return to normal.

Or some semblance of normal.

He rapped on the door, irritated that his thoughts seemed to keep circling his ex.

"Come."

The curt command didn't faze him. Phil was that way with everyone. And, as far as he knew, he hadn't done anything to tick the man off. Not this week, anyway.

He pushed through the door and paused. Someone else was already in there. "Sorry, I can—"

"No, come in. This concerns both of you."

Both?

Taking another look at the chair's occupant, his stomach curdled in protest. Talk about circling. Think about her, and she appeared.

What the hell was Kady doing here?

He'd figured she'd be out lounging by the pool this morning, wearing one of those skimpy bikinis she tended to favor. Memories of creamy skin and long, lithe limbs flashed through his skull, only to be ejected in a hurry.

Not even going there.

That was what had gotten him into trouble in the first place.

He chose to remain standing by the door, even as Phil took his seat again. "You have a group of medical students scheduled to shadow you this week between conference sessions. Are you ready for them?"

Oh, hell, he'd completely forgotten about that. Since most of his workshop responsibilities were in the late afternoons, Phil had asked if a small contingent of students who were interested in obstetrics and pediatrics could follow him on his rounds.

That still didn't explain why Kady was here.

"I am. Thanks for the reminder, though." Even he could hear the tightness in his voice.

Kady was just as tense. He saw it in the stiff set of her spine, in the way her neck was set squarely between her shoulders. And her hands were clutched together, pressed against her belly. A protective posture. Remembered from her pregnancy all those years ago? His own stomach muscles squeezed against each other.

She'd known Phil was going to call him in here.

"Dr. Blacke was going to help originally, but since he can't be here, I thought Dr. McPherson might agree to take his place, since your specialties tie together in some areas. I've been trying to coax her into it. She thinks you might object for some reason. You don't. Correct?"

He waited for Kady to offer up some other kind of excuse, but she just sat there like a stone. It was up to him to derail this train.

"No objections, but I'm sure Dr. McPherson didn't come here expecting to practice medicine."

Phil's glance went from him to Kady. "Can we count on you to help a sister hospital train up a new generation of doctors?"

Leave it to the department head to make it almost impossible to refuse. It was a weapon the man used well.

"Well… Of course. If you think it would help."

The hesitation was obvious. But he knew Phil well enough to know that he would purposely ignore it. And there was no way he could signal her without his boss seeing it.

And Phil wasn't asking anything out of the ordinary. He and Dr. Blacke normally did a kind of back and forth dialogue with medical students.

"Yes, it would help Dr. Stevenson out immensely."

Of course it would.

Tucker was barely able to suppress the eye-roll he

felt coming on. He covered it by asking, "Any idea who will take Gordy's place during his treatment?"

"Not yet. We're still looking for his replacement." He glanced at Kady, a speculative smile curving his lips. "You wouldn't consider transferring to our neck of the woods, would you?"

Kady's hands uncurled and her thumb went to the back of her ring finger and scrubbed at it. Trying to remove any reminders of what was once there? She'd mailed the rings back to him. He still had them somewhere. Why, he had no idea.

"No, I'm sorry. I'm getting ready to—" Her voice came to an abrupt stop, along with her thumb, before starting up again. "I have a lot going on in Atlanta right now. And my family is there."

Kady's grandparents. They were good people who'd raised her after her parents had been killed in a car accident. He respected them. And Kady loved them like crazy. He'd left for New York almost immediately after they'd separated.

He hadn't talked to them about the split. He probably should have faced her grandfather and tried to explain. But what explanation was there, really? He and Kady disagreed on a fundamental part of their life together. She wanted more children. He didn't. Had taken steps to make sure that option was never on the table with Kady, or any another woman.

His and Kady's wants and needs had landed them in opposite corners of the ring, and neither of them was willing to come to the middle.

Middle? There was no middle. One of them would have had to give in completely. He couldn't ask that of Kady. Whispers of guilt surrounded his heart and mind, his teeth clamping tightly to ward them off. She deserved to have kids if that's what she wanted. He just…couldn't. A divorce had seemed better than forcing her to live a life she didn't want. Maybe she already had another child. The thought of that made his jaw lock tight. She wasn't married again, judging from the lack of a ring on that finger she'd been worrying a moment earlier.

Phil nodded. "We'll just have to take whatever you're willing to give while you're here, then. Since Dr. Stevenson is fine with you pairing up, then we're good?"

One side of Tucker's mouth twitched to the side at the way Phil had worded that. He and Kady used to do a whole lot of pairing up—in a completely different sense. There was no way he or Kady were going to admit to that, though, so it looked like they were both stuck. Unless they told Phil they were divorced—from each other—they were going to have a hard time explaining why they couldn't work together.

"I'm happy to help, of course."

Those words were soft. Unsure. Not like the Kady he knew who took the bull by the horns and wrestled it to the ground. Then again, she'd lived through a lot of heartache since their youthful days when they'd been carefree and crazy in love.

"Good. I'll leave you two to work on coordinating your schedules. I appreciate you giving us some of your time, Dr. McPherson. If you go down to HR, they can reimburse you for your hours. Not as much as you'd get for practicing medicine, but we do have a small budget for consultants."

"It's okay. I'm taking Dr. Blacke's place at the conference anyway. If it will help patients in the future, then it's for a good cause."

"We at Wilson-Ross thank you."

It wasn't like Phil to stand on formalities. Or to suggest that a visiting doctor transfer to his department on a permanent basis. He took a closer look at the man as a tinge of something dark and ugly rose up inside him. He didn't see any overt interest, but Phil was divorced too, and Kady was a beautiful woman.

Even if the man was interested, there was nothing he could do about it. Nothing he *would* do about it. His ring was no longer on her finger. She could do as she pleased.

And if Phil pleased her?

Give it a rest, idiot!

Maybe interpreting Phil's words as a dismissal, his ex climbed to her feet and reached to shake Phil's hand. Her blouse rode up, exposing a sliver of her back in the process.

His fingers curled into his palms.

Damn.

How he'd loved to explore each ridge and hollow of her spine, his index finger slowly working its way from her neck all the way down the vertebral column, whispering the names and numbers of each in her ear. By the time he'd reached the bottom, she'd been shaking with need.

So had he.

Sex between them had always been volcanic. Greedy and generous. Two words not normally associated with each other, but that described their lovemaking perfectly.

"Thanks for the opportunity," she murmured.

The opportunity to spend more of her time with her ex? Of course not. That was just his feverish brain lusting after what it couldn't have. What it *shouldn't* have.

Which was why he'd had to let her go two years ago. His body had never listened to his head where she was concerned. If he'd stayed, he would have ended up making them both miserable. He'd seen it in her face. Heard it in her voice.

He waited for her to leave the room, then threw a nod to Phil and followed her out. He fell into step beside her. "You don't have to do this, you know. If you said no, Phil would have to understand."

"And what would we tell him exactly?"

"We'd think of something."

She sighed. "I think it's already been decided. Besides, I want to do it."

"Why?" He was genuinely curious. The last thing they should do was spend any more time than necessary together. Hadn't he already proven that a minute ago? Or maybe she wasn't still as affected by him as he was by her.

"I don't know exactly. It's an exciting chance to see how things are done at the main campus of Wilson-Ross."

"Trust me. It's the same as Wilson-Ross in Atlanta."

"Maybe, but we follow protocols set by New York. You see the first new wave of treatments."

He nodded. "You could get that by meeting with the folks in Maternal-Fetal. I could set up a face to face with them, if you want."

"I would love that. But I'd still like to help with the medical students." She turned her face to look at him. "Unless it would make you too uncomfortable."

That was exactly what he had been thinking just moments earlier. But it wasn't something he wanted to admit. Not even to himself.

"And you wouldn't be?"

The colorful lines on the white linoleum floor helped guide patients and staff alike to different sections of the hospital. He followed the blue stripe, although he knew the route by heart. His office was on the other side of the hospital.

"We've lived through things that were a lot worse than a few hours of awkwardness."

"Yes. We have." He hesitated. It was none of his business, but he had to ask. "Did you ever have more kids?"

Her face paled for a few telling seconds before turning a bright pink. She opened her mouth. Closed it. Then opened it again. "No. I haven't."

"I'm sorry, I shouldn't have asked that."

She stopped in her tracks, her chin popping up. "No. You shouldn't have." Then her face softened. "Thank you for sending the flowers, though."

He didn't have to ask what she was talking about. The monthly daisies for Grace's grave. "The florist sends them. I just put in the order."

"I thought they were from you, but there is never any card attached."

"Grace can't read a card." His jaw tightened again. "Or anything else."

The florist had told him that daisies symbolized innocence and purity. Exactly what he thought of when he remembered his daughter. It had made the suffering she'd gone through all the more terrible somehow.

"Then why send them?" The question didn't have

the challenging tone he would have expected. Instead, she seemed to be searching for something.

He had no idea what, and even if he did, Tucker didn't have an answer for her. He had no idea why he sent them. It was true. Grace would never see or touch or bury her face in those white petals. A tightness gripped his throat that wouldn't let go.

That first trip to the florist's shop had been hard. He'd sat in the parking lot for almost an hour before he'd been able to make himself go inside. The woman at the desk had taken his order, the compassion on her face almost his undoing. But once it was done, it had become almost a ritual—a sacred remembrance of what she'd meant to him.

He shrugged. "I know she would have liked them. It's the only explanation I have."

As she turned to start walking, something made him snag her wrist and pull her to a stop. When she turned to face him again, he took a moment to study her before letting go of her hand. She'd lost weight in the last two years. She wasn't emaciated, by any means, but there were hollows to her cheeks that hadn't been there when they'd been together. Maybe it was because her hair was longer than it had been, those vibrant red waves throwing shadows across her face. But whatever it was, her green eyes were the same, glowing…alive. Only now they were a little more secretive than they used to be. He didn't like not being able to read her the way he once could.

"Are you…?"

Her brows puckered. "Am I what?"

"Are you okay with me sending them? The flowers, I mean." He'd set out to ask her if she was really and truly okay. But since he wasn't sure he really wanted to know, he'd changed it at the last second.

"Yes." Kady reached out and touched his hand. "I think it's sweet. And Nanna and Granda' like seeing them when they go to visit her grave."

"How are they?" Kady's Irish grandparents had taken some getting used to. As had her extended family, which was huge. And loud. And fun. He and his parents had been close, but their family gatherings had been small, reserved affairs. And as an only child, Tucker had learned to imitate that…to remain quiet and stoic no matter what was happening around him.

Not the McPhersons. They all wore their hearts on their sleeves, holding nothing in.

Only Kady did. At least, the Kady standing in front of him did.

She dropped her hand to her side. The urge to reach down and enfold it in his came and went. "They miss Grace, obviously, just like I do. But they're doing okay. Nanna has been a bit forgetful recently, which has Granda' worried."

"Anything serious?"

"I don't think so. I don't see the signs of Alzheimer's there. But time will tell. If it gets worse, I'll talk her into getting some tests."

"A very smart idea."

Tell them I said hi. Send them my love. Tell them I'll see them soon.

None of those responses were appropriate anymore. And it set up an ache inside him that wouldn't quit.

"They're thinking of selling the house and getting something smaller."

The McPhersons' home was huge by any standards.

They'd held large family gatherings there. Thanksgiving. Christmas. Any holiday had been an occasion to be celebrated. He couldn't picture them living anywhere else. The family's wealth had been another thing that had come between him and Kady at the end. She had insisted her grandparents were willing to hire a fertility expert to make sure the odds of having another baby with Tay-Sachs were as low as possible. He'd been dead set against it. Not because of the money it would take. Her grandparents could afford all of that and more. His argument had been more along the lines of not being able to guarantee with a hundred percent certainty that they would not have another child like Grace.

"That would take some getting used to for them, wouldn't it?"

"I think they're ready for a change."

Just like Tucker had been. Looking back, though, he wondered if it wasn't so much that he had been ready for change as it was that he'd been running from his grief. The hopeful look on Kady's face whenever she'd spoken of another baby had been enough to send an icepick through his heart. Eventually the organ had become a sieve, any emotional involvement leaking away until there had been nothing left.

"I hope it all works out for them."

"Thank you."

And on that note it was time for him to get back to his own retooled life. "Well, I have a surgery today at two. I'm assuming the medical students will be coming tomorrow, since Phil didn't mention them being at the hospital today." He paused. "Do you need anything while you're here?"

He wasn't sure what he would do if she came up with something personal.

"No. I think I'm good. I guess I'll see you later this afternoon, if you're in any of the sessions."

"I'm scheduled for the anesthesia and pregnancy track."

She nodded. "I'm not in that one. I have 'Monitoring the High-Risk Pregnancy from Beginning to Delivery.' So I guess I'll see you tomorrow, then. Any idea at all when we're supposed to meet the students?"

He hadn't thought to ask, although Phil had probably told him at some point. "I'm not sure. I'll get hold of him and give you a call at the hotel, if that's okay."

"Yes. I'm in room 708. You can leave a message if I'm not there."

No offer of her cellphone number. But then again, he'd told her he'd call her at the hotel, so maybe she thought he didn't want it.

He didn't.

Did he?

Hell, no. It would just give his fingers an excuse to push and erase those numbers again and again. Or, worse, call her with some trumped-up excuse just so he could hear her voice.

That was all he needed—one more thing to brood over. Not that he'd tried to call her since the divorce. Her cellphone number could be the same, for all he knew.

She said goodbye, and this time when she turned to leave he didn't try to stop her.

Even though there was a small part of him that wanted to do just that.

And he had no idea why.

* * *

Kady had the morning to herself. It was still early and the pool was deserted. Dropping her towel onto a nearby lounger, she went over to the water's edge and dipped in a toe. A shiver rippled over her at the difference in temperature. All the windows were fogged up, but the heat and humidity of the room were a welcome change from the icy interior of the hotel. She kind of liked the misty atmosphere. It gave her a sense of privacy. As if this was her personal luxury spa.

She hadn't seen Tucker at the convention the previous night, but then again they'd been in separate sessions. As soon as her part had ended, she'd gone straight to her room. She'd had a headache, and a dull listlessness had stolen over her, something she hadn't felt in a while. The result of seeing Tucker again?

Probably.

It was a shock, that's all. Anyone in their right mind would feel a big old jolt of disbelief at seeing their ex after all this time.

All this time? It wasn't like it had been ten years since she'd seen him. From her horrified reaction, it might as well have been, though.

And he hadn't called to say what time they were supposed to meet the medical students, so she assumed that wasn't happening until later. Or maybe he'd told Mr. Harold that he preferred she didn't come. That made her frown. She would have expected him to let her know, either way. Unless he'd tried and couldn't reach her.

She probably should have given him her cellphone number, but it hadn't even crossed her mind until she'd been almost out of the hospital. To run back and breathlessly give it to him smacked of teenaged infatuation. And Kady had long since passed those days of young love.

Young love. Ha!

"Cynical, Kady. Cynical."

Okay, it might be cynical, but better that than be hurt by another man. Tucker had talked about never having any more children? Well, she was pretty sure she wasn't getting married again. She hadn't even wanted to date since they'd broken up.

She could just take the plunge and put up a profile on one of those date matcher-upper things. Instead, she took a different kind of plunge and jumped into the pool. The chill shocked her system, almost causing her lungs to contract and blow out all her air reserves. She controlled the urge and then kicked her way to the very bottom. She tooled around, following the downward curve until she reached the deep end. Nice. This was the only kind of plunge she wanted to take. Her eyes burned slightly from the chlorine, but she was used to that. She drifted to where the light was, putting her palm over it before she went even deeper, glancing up at the surface above. She couldn't remember if the pool had an eight- or twelve-foot depth.

What did it matter? She could just stay down here forever.

Except she couldn't.

As they always did, her lungs sent the first twinges of protest to her brain. Just another few seconds.

She closed her eyes and let herself "be." Something she could only seem to do in the water. But her lungs' distress calls had now been taken up by other parts of her body. Time to go. She pushed off the concrete floor and shot toward the light above, breaking the surface and sucking down one huge gulp of air after another, before reaching toward the edge. Instead of a cold tiled surface, she encountered something firm but warm. Curling around her hand.

Blinking the water out of her eyes in a hurry, she glanced up.

"Tucker?" The name rasped across her vocal cords right before shock took control of them and rendered her silent. She wasn't even sure why she'd asked, other than letting her brain in on what her heart already knew: it was him. It had to be, even if the light behind him cast his face in shadow. That, along with his dark jeans and black shirt, gave him a slightly sinister look. He could be a dark god. Or a fallen angel. She couldn't quite decide which fit him better.

Neither.

Breathe, Kady, breathe.

She did just that, trying to figure out if she was just imagining it or if Tucker was really crouched by the side of the pool, gripping her hand. His skin was warm. She could just curl into his palm and...

And nothing.

"I was just about to go in after you."

"You were?"

"You looked pretty lifeless down there. One minute you were swimming like a fish and the next you went into some kind of suspended animation." His thumb made a slight movement across the back of her hand. Small enough to make her wonder if she'd imagined it. Imaginary or not, it sent raw sensation skittering down her nerve endings, making them scramble to interpret it.

There was nothing to interpret.

She struggled to get her tongue to wrap around the words. "You've seen me like that before." He had. Many times.

He paused, fingers tightening slightly on hers. "Yes. I have."

Were they talking about the same thing? "Okay, so you know that I'm fine."

"I do now. You're a land creature, Kady. You belong up here."

Next to him? When he looked like that? When just the touch of his hand on hers was making her picture all kinds of crazy scenarios? Like pulling him into the pool and seeing what it started?

There was no way in hell she was going to do that. "What are you doing here, anyway?"

"I lost the slip of paper with your room number on it." The pad of his thumb shifted again. This time there was no way it was her imagination. Why was he still holding onto her anyway? And why the heck wasn't she pulling away?

"How did you expect to find me when you came over, then?"

"I hadn't thought that far ahead." He smiled. "Want me to help you out?"

She took stock of the situation. Her towel was way over there. And she was dressed in a pretty skimpy bikini. He'd seen her stretch marks and the changes in her abdomen from carrying Grace before. But they'd been married back then. When things between them had been easy and comfortable.

She was no longer comfortable in his presence. She was self-conscious and nervous. And she didn't like it.

Better to just face it. "Sure. Thanks."

She gave a quick kick of her legs to help him, and Tucker hauled her up and out of the pool. His eyes skated across her torso, then he dropped her hand as if he'd grabbed the wrong end of a scalpel. Then he swore, his gaze moving up and out—landing on anything except her.

What the...?

When she glanced down, she shrieked. The side strings on her bikini top had come undone, something she would have noticed had she not been so busy trying to figure out if he was stroking her hand. And getting worked up over it.

Well, she wasn't worked up anymore!

Turning away quickly, thankful now for the fogged-up glass, she yanked the strings behind her back and attempted to tie them. Except she normally turned the top around and tied it in the front before twisting it to the back once more and then knotting the top.

Why couldn't she have worn a one-piece?

Well, she hadn't expected Tucker to walk in on her, for one thing.

Why do you care? The man has seen you naked, for heaven's sake. He's seen you giving birth. He cut the cord afterward.

But that noise he'd just made hadn't been an "Oh, big deal" sound.

It had been more like, "Did I just see what I think I saw?" In the old days, she would have thrown him a sexy quip and invited him closer. Much closer. They then would have spent the next couple of hours tangled in a heap, finding the first available surface. The bed. The sofa. The dining-room table.

On the fourth try with the strings she let out an exasperated breath.

"Do you need help?"

"No." She wasn't going to admit it, even if she did.

"Here, let me."

Warm hands brushed her icy ones aside, fingers gliding across her skin. Prickles broke out, rippling across her body and ending at her nipples, which tightened unbearably.

Because this time the slow, soft touches weren't in her imagination.

Lordy!

She hadn't invited him to come closer, but he had anyway.

It wasn't for the same reasons, but her body thought it was. It was busy rolling out the red carpet for the man while he worked on unaware.

As embarrassing and awkward as her reaction to the workings of his fingers was, it was even worse when he suddenly stopped. "I think that's got it. Do you need it double knotted?"

There was a low roughness to his voice that made her stomach contract. She should tell him, no, that she was fine, that she was done anyway.

"Please."

Was that her head talking? Or her overly eager libido?

She had no idea, only knew that her eyes slid closed as soon as he touched her again. What he didn't know wouldn't hurt him. And, God, she had missed this part of their relationship.

His movements weren't quite as sure as they'd been a few minutes ago. His palm brushed her back, all five fingers trailing down her spine in a way that was burned into her memory. Then his touch was gone.

Was that an accident? Or was that blast from the past done on purpose?

Accident. It had to be.

Snapping herself back to reality, she made sure her boobs were fully contained before turning to face him—praying her errant nipples weren't as prominent as they felt. "So why didn't you just call the hotel and ask them to connect you with my room?"

His gaze was glued to her face as if a single shift might spell disaster. It very well could. For both of them.

"I was right across the street and thought I'd just leave a message at the desk. Then they told me they'd seen you come in here, and I thought I'd tell you in person. I didn't know you'd be…" He gestured toward the pool.

"What else would I be doing in here?" As soon as the words left her mouth, she knew they were a mistake. They'd had a very sexy encounter one time at a private pool at a cabin they'd rented in the mountains.

She gulped. "What was the message?"

"That the medical students will arrive at around ten this morning."

"Ten? *This* morning?" Panic fluttered in her chest. "You just found this out?"

"I did. Phil called, but I wasn't in a position where I could answer, so he left me a voice mail. I assumed he left you one as well." His voice tightened. "I just wanted to make sure."

Tucker hadn't been able to answer his phone when his boss called? Why not?

It was none of her business what he did or didn't do. Except when he barged into where she was swimming and almost gave her a heart attack.

And then made her want him all over again.

At least he didn't know. Or did he?

"I haven't checked with the front desk yet, so maybe he did leave a message."

He glanced at his watch, not quite meeting her eyes. "It doesn't matter. Since it's eight thirty, we have time for you to change and get some breakfast, if you haven't already eaten."

She hadn't, but she wasn't sure she wanted to spend any more time with him than necessary outside the hospital or the conference center. He'd been in close proximity to her for, what? Ten minutes? And those nimble fingers tripping down her spine had set off all kinds of cravings.

A week. It's only a week. Surely you can contain your impulses for seven measly days.

"Good thing you got the message to me, or I might have had to show up to work in my bikini."

Yikes. She'd meant it as a joke, but it didn't sound quite as blasé as she'd hoped it might.

So much for containing her impulses.

"I don't think Phil would approve of drool-lined hallways. Someone might slip and hurt themselves."

That made her smile. "I take it you aren't talking about you?"

He chuckled. "I would be too busy beating them off with a stick to worry about slipping."

"Would you beat them off?"

He was just kidding. He had to be.

"I wouldn't have to. Because you *are* going to

change out of that. Otherwise things are liable to get…
complicated."

A shiver went down her spine at the memory of his
fingers skipping across her skin.

Complicated?

Hell, they already were. If he touched her again,
she'd be the one slipping. As in slipping under his spell
all over again. That would be disastrous for everyone.

She did her best to pass it off with a laugh. "Well,
I'm all about things staying uncomplicated. So I'll go
up and change. And I'll take you up on your breakfast
offer, if it still stands."

"It does."

"Then if I can have fifteen minutes, I'll be back
down in something more suitable for work."

And more suitable to hold herself in line. Although
she wasn't sure she had anything in her suitcase with
the power to do that.

But she was going to have to somehow dredge up a
hefty dose of willpower. Before someone slipped and
went down, like Tucker said they might.

And that someone was most likely to be her.

CHAPTER THREE

THEY ENDED UP taking breakfast back to Tucker's office, while he tried to figure out why he'd gone into
that pool room. But the windows had been fogged up
enough that he hadn't been able to make out anything
inside. He was still shaken by the image of Kady float-
ing in that pool. He'd truly thought something had
happened. His heart had galloped in his chest, and
he'd just reached for the bottom of his shirt to pull it
off when she'd darted full force toward the surface.

That had to be why he'd reacted to her bikini the
way he had. Or rather her wardrobe malfunction.
Thank God it hadn't been the upper strings that had
come loose. It had been bad enough to get that tantalizing glimpse of the lower curve of her breast. His
body had released a sudden rush of endorphins and
brought with it a craving for this woman he'd never
truly figured out how to suppress and he had no idea
why. But he'd better damn well find the page in the in-
struction manual if he was going to survive this week.

At least now she was dressed in tan slacks and a
black scoop-necked top. Very professional. If he'd expected that to be his get-out-of-jail-free card, though,
he was sorely mistaken. Because his memory was just

fine, thank you very much. And it wasn't likely to forget that tiny drop of water that had clung to that exposed strip of flesh. He'd wanted to lick it off. To lay her down on that concrete floor and make love to her. The urge had erupted out of nowhere, shocking him with its intensity. Only it wasn't love.

It was lust. Pure and simple. Their sex life had never lacked for anything.

Until Grace had died. After that he hadn't been able to...

"How's your omelet?" Kady's voice broke through his thoughts.

He forced a brow up as if he hadn't a care in the world. "It's hospital food. How do you think it is?"

"My mixed fruit is pretty good."

"Because it only requires chopping. The fruit does all the work as far as taste goes."

"Which is why I chose it."

Although his office was fairly large and comfortable, it felt the size of a cramped work cubicle at the moment. Kady was perched on his leather sofa...the same one he normally stretched out on when he put in long hours, snatching bits of sleep when he could.

He'd put plenty of space between them. At least he'd thought he had. But even though she was on the sofa and he was on a nearby chair, he could still see a tiny vein that pulsed at the base of her throat, could enjoy the way her brows puckered and moved as she talked. The way she moistened her lips when she paused to collect her thoughts.

He recognized it all. Recognized the slight lilt from her Irish roots. Not an accent per se, just a slightly different rise and fall to her voice than most Americans had. A carryover from living with her grandparents.

Forcing a smile, he decided to change the subject. Put it firmly back in the business court. "So, Phil said there are thirteen medical students who'll be joining us. We'll head to Maternity and look over the cases down there first, and then head up to the surgical unit."

"Okay, tell me what I need to do."

"Well, one of my cases yesterday came about after an ultrasound uncovered a problem with a fetus's digestive tract, and the patient's OB/GYN called me. A section of the abdominal wall hadn't closed properly, allowing the baby's intestines to slide outside of the body."

She leaned forward, her interest obvious. "Were you able to close it? How old was the fetus?"

"The mother was thirty-three weeks along and, yes, I was able to close it." He paused. "That's where we can help these students see how certain specialties work together. If you'd come across a similar ultrasound, would you have referred the patient to a surgeon?"

"I'd have to look at all the data but, yes, if it was as straightforward as you say, I would have called you in as soon as we spotted it."

"Good. That's what Phil was looking for, I think. To show them how cases can flow back and forth between doctors."

"I see. Is there anything in the maternity department right now that might land in your court?"

He allowed himself to relax slightly. "Nothing at the moment. But we're going to concentrate on high-risk pregnancies and talk about when surgical intervention is considered and why."

"That sounds pretty straightforward."

"It's actually hard for me to think like a medical student these days. Is it the same for you?"

Kady's lips twisted to one side for a moment as if she was thinking. "I think so, although I probably haven't had as much contact with students as you do here in New York."

"We were so young back then, weren't we?"

Back when passion had been without thought, and he hadn't had to worry about whether or not he would ever make love to a woman again. That fear had turned into a self-fulfilling prophecy, which in turn had sparked a vicious cycle. Even the thought of trying caused acid to churn in his stomach and made his heart pound in his chest. He lived in dread of intimate glances or, worse, a candlelit dinner. Those days had been one endless nightmare.

In the end, his problem had been all in his head. The vasectomy had both cured him and doomed him.

"As if you're ancient now."

"Sometimes I feel like it." And if that wasn't the truth, he didn't know what was.

She took a bite of one of the strawberries on her plate and took her time chewing and swallowing before speaking again. "So do I. But I think that's the long hours talking. This conference is actually like a mini-vacation to me."

"So I saw."

Perfect. He was back to the bikini scene. Leave it to his mind to somehow find its way to the very place he didn't want it to go. And there had been no hint of his

body hesitating at what it had seen. It had wanted it.
Wanted her. What he wouldn't have given for that back
when they'd been together. But that hadn't happened.
His mind had wanted her, but his body had been too
paralyzed by fear to respond to his mental commands.
The humiliation had been crushing. Damning.

From all appearances, those days were over.

"Hey, it's a hotel. I don't always have access to a
pool. I looked up the amenities and came prepared."

"You always were good at that."

She smiled. "Not always. That's how we wound
up with Grace."

His entire body chilled in an instant. Yes. It was
how they'd wound up with Grace. He'd often wondered
whether, if he could have seen the future, he would
have chosen for her not to be born.

His innards wound tight, clenching and releas-
ing. Would he? He couldn't imagine never seeing
that sweet baby's smile. Never feeling her tiny fingers clamp onto his. And there was his answer. He
wouldn't change it. Even though the agony of those
days was still almost impossible to look back on without deep sadness.

Kady must have sensed the change in him because
she set her plate down next to her hip and leaned
across to touch his wrist. "It wasn't your fault, Tucker.
It wasn't either of our fault. We were in a hurry. We
were young and in love. We'd been talking about marriage from the time of our second date. The pregnancy
just fast-forwarded all of those plans."

Did she think he was upset that they'd gotten married because of the baby? He never regretted marrying
her. What he did wish was that they'd known about

the possibility of Tay-Sachs right from the beginning. And he wished he'd talked to her after Grace had died about what was going on in his head.

It would have solved nothing, though.

"There's no way we can change any of it, so it doesn't really matter."

"Would you, if you could?"

At the look of hurt on her face, he frowned, realizing how brusque he'd sounded. But when she moved to pull back, his fingers lightly encircled her wrist, holding her in place. "I don't know, Kady. It's not something I would choose to go through a second time." He'd made sure he wouldn't. And he didn't regret it. Not for a second.

"I don't think any of us would."

And yet she'd wanted another baby, despite the possibility that it could happen a second time. Was it probable? No. But the slim chance that it could tied his stomach in knots, making it impossible to make love to her. What if she'd accidentally gotten pregnant a second time? Part of the reason he'd pulled back emotionally had been because of that. And part of it had been that he'd just been unable to perform, knowing that any type of birth control could fail. Any except for one.

"It's over and done with." And so were they. Yet seeing her in that pool had coaxed a reaction from his body that he hadn't been able to manage for the last year of their marriage.

Why now? Why not back then?

Was she dating anyone? It was none of his business, but it would be a lot easier to resist the tug and pull of need if she was. His gaze dropped to her stomach.

What would it be like to see her swollen with some-one else's child?

A faceless form appeared in his head, only to have Tucker kick it away as hard as he could.

Thank God that wasn't something he would ever have to witness.

She tugged her wrist free from his grip. "You're right. It is."

"Kady." This time it was he who leaned forward. "I never wanted it to end the way it did."

"The fact that you filed for divorce says you did."

His gaze raked her face. "You gave me no option."

"'There are always options to be explored.' Isn't that what you said at the workshop that first night?"

He shook his head. "You wanted another child. I didn't."

"You made that rather obvious."

Hot air stuck in his lungs. Was she talking about how he'd avoided the bedroom?

She went on, "When you moved into the guest room, I figured a divorce was inevitable."

He had moved out of their bedroom. But he hadn't had much of a choice. It had been either that or have her discover his secret. And add one more thing to her plate? Kady had always been good at blaming herself.

So was he.

"We were both dealing with so much at the time." They had been. Decisions that had been impossible to make under the weight of grief. "I wanted to give us both some space."

"You succeeded. We had a whole lot of space. And not just in terms of the bedroom."

"I know. Maybe we can get off to a fresh start."

"Fresh start?" She met his eyes. "What do you mean?"

"We were once friends. Maybe we could start there."

Friends. Was he kidding?

"What makes you think that's even possible?"

Tucker propped a foot on his left knee. "Because we're mature adults. We've both moved on with our lives. We should be able to let the past go, right?"

They should. Except that her sitting across from him was sending messages to all the wrong parts of his body. Parts that were definitely showing signs of functioning around her again.

"We've never made very good friends, Tucker."

She was right. The sex had always been too intense. So crazy hot that they hadn't been able to stop and nurture some of the deeper stuff.

"No. We didn't, did we?"

And there it was. That glitter of green eyes that said she knew exactly what he was talking about.

"Nope. But I don't remember either of us complaining about it." Their gazes locked, her tongue peeking out to moisten her lips. And suddenly there was a familiar pressure behind his zipper and a big old hole where common sense should have been.

His body was functioning, but right now he needed it to take a few deep breaths and hit pause before they wound up somewhere they would both regret. "No, we didn't. But maybe we should have."

She reeled back slightly in her seat. "I'm sorry?"

"I didn't mean that the way it sounded. I just want us to tread carefully. You're here for a week. I don't want to do something that I can't undo."

The image of that undone bikini top wandered through his head before he pushed it aside.

"I don't either. So what are you proposing?"

"That we use self-discipline. Self-control. The very things that carried us through medical school. Surely we can do that."

Not that Kady hadn't shown both of those things. But since he was the one who seemed to be struggling, maybe he needed to voice the words to give her fair warning.

"That sounds reasonable. But maybe you should stay away from the pool from now on."

He smiled. "For once, we're in agreement."

"Shake on it?" She held out her hand.

As he rose to his feet and moved over to do as she asked, he hoped he could remember what he'd said. And start practicing a little of that self-discipline he seemed to be lacking.

"Well, now that that's settled—" he let go of her hand "—shall we go down to the maternity ward and see what cases they have?"

She'd thought he was going to kiss her a moment or two ago. And she wouldn't have stopped him. Her lungs had greedily held onto every scrap of air, just in case.

And then he'd shut the whole thing down with a single line.

A little voice whispered that it was for the best. Of course it was. But that didn't mean her body agreed with that voice. Or even listened to it. Ever. At least not where Tucker was concerned. She should be glad he'd come to his senses. Because she sure hadn't come to hers.

Smoothing her blouse down and waiting for him to gather what he needed off his desk, she tried to get her errant heart and her crazed thoughts back under control. There was nothing to worry about. Tucker was just taking precautions.

But she was worried. Maybe not about him but about herself. How easy it would have been to slide back into his arms. To forget all the pain and heartache that had happened between them.

But he was right. Once it happened, there would be no undoing it.

"Ready?" He glanced back, his hand on the door lever.

"Yes."

Please, let's go out and rejoin the real world, where exes don't fantasize about each other. At least, they shouldn't.

People streamed up and down the corridor, lanyards designating some as staff, while others were either patients or visitors. The hospital was busier than the one in Atlanta, but at least it gave her a chance to catch her breath. Not easy with Tucker's tight haunches and broad shoulders striding ahead of her. His phone pinged twice, but the messages couldn't have been important because he glanced down and then kept walking, not bothering to respond.

Or maybe he didn't want her to know who they were from.

Ridiculous.

It didn't matter one way or the other. He didn't have a ring on, though, so he hadn't remarried. And she knew him well enough to know there was no way he would have hinted about things happening between them if he was involved with someone.

A minute later they joined several people in front of the elevator. "What floor is the maternity ward on?"

"Third. The surgical department is here on the fifth floor, which is where I spend the bulk of my time."

She cocked her head and said in a low voice, "Is it hard to do the surgeries?"

"What do you mean?"

A quick shrug as she tried to blow away the impulsive question. Then the doors to the elevator opened. They waited for those who were getting off to do so, before moving into the cabin. It was a quick trip, since they only had to go down two floors. Then they were in the lobby of the maternity unit where a huge sign over the main door gave the department's mission statement:

To give every pregnant woman who crosses the Wilson-Ross threshold the safest, most respectful birthing experience possible.

She paused. It was worded differently than the one at her hospital, which was interesting. She had assumed both hospitals would be cookie-cutter versions of each other, but that wasn't the case. She was already seeing subtle differences. The way the hospitals were laid out. The decor was individual as well, probably to reflect the flavor of the host city.

Tucker paused by one of the doors. "Yes. Sometimes it's hard to do the surgeries. Especially when it's a case where genetics are involved." He glanced at her. "But then there are those days when everything just falls into place and I feel like I'm doing what I wasn't able to do for Grace—give a baby a chance for a normal life."

"Oh, Tucker…" She paused, trying to gather her thoughts. "I feel the same way. There are times I think I see her, when I'll pass a child's room and see what I think are Grace's blond hair and blue eyes."

"I know."

He really did know.

She touched his arm and went to say something else when a bustle of movement caught her eye as they turned a corner. The pace on the floor was frenetic, which might have been normal, except for the… Her vision sharpened as nurses rushed from room to room, and several alarms beeped at the unattended nurses' desk. Her grip tightened on his arm as a sliver of fear went through her. "Is it always this way?"

"No." He stopped the nearest nurse. "What's going on?"

"There was a fire at the Heritage Birthing Center a few streets over. Ten patients in various stages of labor are either here or on their way over."

Kady let go of Tucker's arm, her chest tightening. She knew all too well the pain, fear and confusion some of those women were experiencing. She'd felt the same panicked helplessness firsthand, which was why she'd specialized in this area of medicine. And yet it was an area in which there was at least hope for a good outcome. Unlike with Grace.

She took a step forward. "I'm a maternal-fetal doctor from Wilson-Ross in Atlanta. Tell me how I can help."

Tucker nodded as well. "We'll both help. Put us where you need us."

CHAPTER FOUR

THE BABY'S HEAD finally crowned. Three hours of pushing had exhausted the young mother, whose chart said she was just seventeen years old. Tucker had thought for sure that Kady was going to order a C-section, but instead she had manually maneuvered the baby several times, the patient groaning in agony with each attempt. She'd arrived at the hospital in the pushing stage, too close to delivery to attempt an epidural unless they were going to take the baby.

"You're almost there, Samantha. Deep breaths and rest until the next contraction."

Kady's face was beaded with perspiration, and fatigue rimmed her eyes. This was the fourth delivery they had assisted with, having had to leave this patient to attend others who had given birth quicker than their current patient.

Picking up a cup from a nearby table, he offered Kady a sip from the straw so she wouldn't need to swap out her gloves after touching the glass. She leaned forward and pulled a couple of long drinks of cold water, nodding her thanks up at him.

She had always been good with her patients, empathy mixing with skill. It was the perfect combination in any physician, but it was even more valuable in an obstetrician.

Did these deliveries seem mundane to her, since she was used to dealing with the sickest of the sick? If so, there was no evidence of it in her face.

The patient moaned. "It's starting again."

She had no one with her, whether it was because of the fire or just because she was alone in this thing, he had no idea. There hadn't been any next of kin listed on her chart, and Kady probably didn't want to put any unnecessary stress on her by asking about a significant other.

He imagined Kady all alone, raising a child, and a rock formed in his stomach. She had been such a great mother to Grace, but it was something they'd shared in together. To do it all by herself... There were women like Samantha, though, who did it all the time—from birth to high-school graduation and beyond. Kady would at least have her grandparents. But if her grandmother really was beginning to lose her memory, how long would she be able to count on her?

If Kady decided to have a child, she'd do it with someone. Wouldn't she?

"Okay, Samantha, take a deep breath and bear down."

That was Tucker's cue to count. Banishing everything else from his mind, he laid a hand on the patient's shoulder and did just that, counting down the seconds and letting his ex do her job without interference from him.

Not that he would. This was her area of expertise. His was in infants far smaller than this one. "Ten. Deep breath and go again."

Samantha's face turned red as she continued to push, pulling up on her legs, limbs trembling with effort.

"Head's out. Stop pushing."

"I—I can't. I have to…"

Tucker stepped into her line of vision. "Blow through it, Samantha. You can do it." He huffed along with her, knowing that Kady was working to make sure the shoulders could be eased out. Tears streamed down the girl's face, tugging at something in his chest. Samantha had red hair, much like Kady's, and it brought back memories from years earlier of Grace's birth. He shoved those thoughts from his mind in a rush.

"Okay, we're ready. Not much longer, Samantha."

He guided her through counting once more, praying Kady was right.

Two more pushes and then a thin cry drifted his way. Samantha's head fell back to the pillow, eyes closed as she struggled to catch her breath.

A nurse brought the baby up to the young mother, easing her gown aside to allow the skin-to-skin contact that the birthing center would have wanted. Wilson-Ross did this as well if mothers requested it, but sometimes traditional methods were slower to change. Kind of like the difference between turning a barge and turning a speedboat. The smaller operations were able to make those shifts in methodology a lot quicker than a bigger hospital could. But sometimes there were trade-offs to be made.

Kady was still working on delivering the afterbirth evidently, but when he looked over at her, he noted the tight white lines on either side of her mouth immediately. Something was wrong.

He glanced back at the mother, who, although she had one arm around the baby's back, was very quiet. Too quiet.

Then he saw a splash of blood on the floor just as Kady raised the alarm. "I have a PPH here! I need two large-bore IV lines started."

Postpartum hemorrhage.

The two nurses both went into action, one removing the baby from the mother's arms and carrying her over to a nearby table. The staff was already bare bones because of the added caseload from the birthing center, so Tucker jumped to help, checking the chart for blood type and calling down to get the wheels turning. He then called the surgical department, in case they needed to take the patient in for emergency surgery.

The urge to take over bubbled up inside him, but he held back, knowing that Kady was well qualified to call the shots. He couldn't stop his head from going through the steps he would take, though, were this his case.

The patient's eyes were now closed, face much paler than it should have been. Dammit. How much blood was she losing?

"Tucker, I need fluids and Pitocin pushed. I want to try to close off these vessels."

"On it. Can you see what's causing it?"

"Not yet. Looking now."

He let her work, another nurse coming in to get the baby and take it to the nursery. Lines were started with the Pitocin drip. If they could get the uterus to contract down on the leaking vessels they might be able to avert a catastrophe. "Do you want me to apply pressure manually?"

Sometimes massaging the abdomen would also help encourage the body to get back on track.

"Yes."

He applied deep rhythmic massage to the area over the uterus, glad that the woman was unconscious. After five minutes his forearms began to burn. Kady was still working feverishly, trying to figure out what was causing the bleeding.

"It's slowing."

Relief filtered through his system. "Do we need a couple of units of blood? They're standing by with some."

"Give me another minute. If I can get it stopped, we may be good with just the fluids."

"Do you want me to keep going?"

"Yes. I'll take whatever help I can get."

There had been a time when he had prayed that very prayer to a God who'd remained silent. In the end, Grace's condition had remained unchanged, and she'd died.

Was life really that arbitrary?

He wasn't sure, but he was glad that in this case things seemed to be turning around.

"Okay, I think we're close to normal levels. Let's stop and see what we've got."

Tucker halted his manipulations and waited, as did the nurse who was working to keep track of times and vitals. Silence enveloped the room as they waited for Kady to either set them back in motion or call off the alarm.

"Still holding. Let's ease up on the Pitocin and see if things continue. Is she conscious?"

"No." He and the nurse said the word together.

"Let's get a blood count so we can see how much volume she has left."

During pregnancy, a woman's blood volume increased by about fifty percent, so some bleeding was normal. It was just when it went beyond a certain level that it turned into a crisis. At its worst, they would have had to perform a hysterectomy in order to save the mother's life. Thankfully it hadn't come to that.

It was as if the lab had been waiting right outside. Or maybe the pediatric nurse had alerted them, because they were there in less than thirty seconds.

Samantha's eyelids fluttered as they were doing the blood draw.

A few minutes later they had their answer. The red-cell count was low, but not dangerously so. With the help of the two nurses, he and Kady worked to clean her up and make her as comfortable as possible.

"Can I see my baby?" The patient's voice was a mere whisper. "Is she all right?"

Kady came around and held her hand. "She's fine. You're the one who gave us a little scare. I can let you see her, but just for a few minutes. I want to send you to ICU for observation to make sure the bleeding doesn't start back up again."

"What caused it?"

"When the placenta detaches it can cause some bleeding, which is normal. You just lost more than we expected. You were also pushing for a long time. The important thing is that your body was able to do what it needed to do to stop it."

"What about the baby? Can she go with me?"

"To ICU? No, I'm sorry. But I'm hoping you'll be able to have her with you before the night is out. I'll check on you periodically to see how you're doing."

That made Tucker frown. She'd already been working for six hours straight. And she wasn't even a resident at this hospital. She could very easily turn the case over to another doctor.

But that wasn't the Kady he knew. She cared deeply about her patients, even ones she hadn't followed through the prenatal phase.

When he went to say something, though, she gave a quick shake of her head. She'd evidently known exactly where he was headed. It was fine. The hospital was undoubtedly glad to have her on hand during this crisis. And because she worked at a sister hospital, it made the process a little more fluid than it might have been otherwise.

"I'll get the nurse to bring your baby in to you for a few minutes."

"Can I nurse her?"

Kady paused as if thinking. "Yes, I think that might be a good idea, actually, if you're feeling strong enough."

Nursing was another way to trigger the body to clamp down on the uterus, signaling that childbirth was over and it was time to close up shop.

The baby latched on without difficulty, and Kady smiled and squeezed Samantha's shoulder. "We'll be right over here, if you need us."

She wasn't going to step out of the room, not while her patient needed her.

"I can stay with her," Tucker said. "Why don't you take a break?"

"I'm fine. I'd rather be on hand."

He smiled. "You always were stubborn."

"No more stubborn than you."

The urge to put his arm around her and give her a quick hug came and went. Not smart, Tucker. You're colleagues now, remember? Nothing more. What he felt right now, though, went far beyond professional admiration. Kady's calm determination had been one of the things he'd loved about her. She never gave up.

Not even when it came to wanting another baby.

"Good job, by the way. I thought for sure she was going to need more aggressive measures."

"I did too. I just wanted to give her body another minute or two to figure things out."

The process for a PPH was similar to resuscitating a cardiac patient. It was a tense situation that could quickly deteriorate into a life-threatening emergency. Tucker had seen a woman die from blood loss. Not common in this day and age of emergency surgery, but when a patient arrived who had already lost over half her blood volume, there sometimes wasn't enough time to reverse things. Thankfully it had only happened once in his memory, but since he didn't deal with this end of things very often, it could occur more than he'd thought.

"You made the right call."

"This time. You're never quite sure when things are happening so quickly."

He knew what she meant. Sometimes you had to go with your gut instincts, because there wasn't time to think through every remote possibility. Had his gut instinct been wrong about getting a vasectomy?

It was too late to do anything about it now. He could see now that his head hadn't been screwed on straight during Grace's last days or afterward. He'd been operating on a ball of pure emotion and grief, while doing his best to hide both of those things from his wife. Not exactly the best conditions under which to make decisions.

It hadn't been a rash one, though. He'd wanted to save his marriage—had hoped that by having the procedure they could have normal relations again. Instead, he'd ended up sending a wrecking ball straight into it.

Divorce had seemed inevitable by then. They had wanted different things out of life.

No, not out of life. Out of one area of that life. She wanted more kids, and he didn't. And the fear of her getting pregnant again messed with a certain region of his brain, which in turn shut down an important region of his body.

"I think the baby's done."

Their patient's quiet voice called him back from his thoughts. Kady had been silent as well. Had she been thinking about the past? Probably not. She'd been able to move on quite easily after the divorce. And she certainly hadn't seemed brokenhearted during the workshop. Or afterward. Shocked to see him maybe. But distraught. Not hardly.

Even the bikini mishap hadn't seemed to faze her, unlike Tucker, who'd almost turned her around to see if that part of his body could follow through to completion.

Another line of thought he needed to stay away from.

Samantha gave her baby one last kiss on the forehead, her eyes filling with tears, before allowing her to be wheeled away in her bassinet. "It's so hard to let her go."

A pang went through him. At least Samantha was only handing her daughter over on a temporary basis. Not letting her go forever.

"It's not for long. We want her to leave with a strong and healthy mom." Kady's words rang with a sincerity that made a believer out of him. There was no hint of remembered grief in her voice. "Let me check you one more time before we have you transferred."

The gloves snapped off a few seconds later. "The flow looks normal."

"Does that mean I can just go to a regular room?"

"Let's play it safe, okay? It'll just be for a few hours. You don't have anyone you want to call?"

Okay, so Kady was going to ask. He'd wondered.

Samantha shrugged. "My roommate, maybe, but she's at work until midnight."

"Do you know her number?"

Once Kady had written it down, she tucked it into her pocket. "We'll see if we can reach her."

We? A figure of speech, surely. She wasn't looking to spend more time with him than she already had. They'd worked these cases together for almost seven straight hours. She had to be dead on her feet.

He was tired too, but that didn't necessarily mean he wanted to go home. Sometimes the rush of adrenaline needed to carry you through a difficult case also made it hard to sleep when the time came. He just wanted to go and get something to eat and get away from the noise of the hospital for a while.

They got their patient prepped and an orderly came up to wheel her to ICU. "I'll check on you a little later tonight."

Surely she wasn't planning on staying at the hospital all night? Then again, knowing Kady...

With their patient gone, Tucker surveyed the room, still cluttered with the evidence of their battle. "I certainly didn't expect the night to end this way."

"It's not over yet. I need to see if they need help with any other cases."

When she went to leave the room, he stopped her with a touch. "What you need to do is take a breather."

"I'm okay. Seriously. I'm just happy to be useful."

"I thought you were taking a mini-vacation."

"Sometimes things are taken out of your hands." She paused. "I needed this, Tucker."

He could agree with that. Sometimes things were taken out of your hands, even when those hands tried to hold on as tightly as they could.

"If you're going to insist on staying, I'll go with you. I probably couldn't sleep anyway."

Strangely, after some of his most devastating cases, he had come home and held Kady all through the night. She'd never asked for details about what had happened, just hugged him back, maybe sensing that's what he'd needed more than anything. Those days were gone. It was one of the things he missed the most about their life together. He doubted he'd find that kind of intimacy with another person.

But he wouldn't find it with her either. Not now. A wisp of regret curled through his skull, searching for a place to land. He hardened his heart. He didn't need intimacy. Not when it involved losing a piece of your soul.

The earlier chaos in the hallway had died down considerably. They had changed shifts somewhere in the middle of it. He went over to the nurses' station where one of the regular RNs, Gloria Luther, was tapping away at a computer keyboard. "Any other cases from the birthing center?"

"I think yours was the last one. Thanks for your help, Dr. Stevenson, and…" She slid her glasses a little further down her nose and sent a glance to Kady. "Things have been so busy I didn't even get a chance to learn your name. I take it you are a real doctor."

Kady laughed. "About as real as they come."

"This is Dr. McPherson from Wilson-Ross in Atlanta. She's here for the conference and is helping orient some of our medical students so you'll be seeing her from time to time this week."

"Nice to meet you." The woman reached across the top of the desk to shake her hand. "And great timing, by the way."

With graying hair scraped back in a severe knot and a gruff appearance, this was one case where appearances were deceptive. Gloria was one of their patients' favorite nurses. She didn't put up with any nonsense but would stand toe to toe with any doctor who wasn't moving quickly enough to help those in her care.

"Thank you." Kady smiled at her.

The nurse looked at her a little longer than necessary and then back at Tucker, before saying, "Oh, I see."

"I'm sorry?" he said, frowning.

"Nothing. You've been at the Atlanta hospital for a while?" she asked Kady.

"I've been there ever since graduating from medical school."

"I think Dr. Stevenson came from that same hospital, didn't you?" She sent him a sly glance. "Did you know each other there?"

You could say that. But he wasn't about to admit they were ex-spouses, although if she went looking on the internet, he was pretty sure there would be pictures of the two of them together at some of the Atlanta hospital's functions. Back when they had probably still been smiling.

Kady saved him from answering. "Yes, we knew each other. We were married for a while, actually."

His gut sucked tight. Why had she admitted that? Gloria wasn't known for being part of the rumor mill, but word could still get around and make things awkward for both of them.

"I thought maybe that was the case. Well, at least you can get along well enough to still work together. My ex and I aren't nearly as lucky."

It was lucky, wasn't it? They weren't ranting and raving at each other, and he was pretty sure Kady didn't actively hate him, although she'd probably felt pretty strongly about him when he'd filed for divorce. But all of that had to be looked at based on where they'd been in their lives at the time.

And that had been in separate bedrooms.

Grief combined with fear of discovery was a potent combination, he'd found out. In all the wrong ways.

"I'm not sure I would call it lucky." Kady threw a

smile at the other woman. "But being angry doesn't do either of us any good."

He well remembered that anger…and the pleading. But neither had changed his mind.

Nothing had. And he still didn't regret his decision. It had given back a part of him that he'd feared dead. Not that he'd slept with many women in the years since the divorce, but at least he knew he could, if he wanted to.

And with Kady at the pool? Oh, yeah, he'd wanted to.

"Well, I'm happy for you. You put in a long shift together, from what I heard. And you both came through it alive." She sent them a quick smile.

Yes, it really had been a long day. And those words brought back the bone-weary tiredness he'd been struggling with for the last half-hour. Maybe he'd be able to sleep after all. "Yes, it was. You're sure that was the last case from the birthing center?"

"Yes. It looks like it's going to be a quiet night from here on out. Our beds are full from the new arrivals, but we should be able to cope."

"Any losses?"

"No, thank God."

Samantha Peters had probably been the closest call they'd had. And Kady had handled it all like the pro she was.

"We're going to take off, then." He paused, realizing something. "We missed the evening's conference sessions."

Kady shrugged. "It's fine." Then she glanced at the board to the right, where a long string of names and room numbers were listed. "I want to be kept updated on Samantha Peters, if you don't mind. I'll be in to check on her around midnight."

Gloria wrote something down. "Will you be close by?"

When his ex looked flustered for a moment, Tucker stepped in. "She will. I'll set her up in my office."

"Okay." She glanced at the board in front of her. "Room 301's call button just went off, so that's my signal to skedaddle. If you'll leave your number on the desk, I'll let you know if anything changes."

How would the nurse even know if there were changes since Samantha had been transferred out of the unit?

"She's not in Maternity anymore—she's in ICU."

Gloria's brows went up. "You're not the only one who likes to check on their patients' progress. I'll call up to ICU from time to time and see how she's doing."

"Thank you."

With that Gloria hurried toward a room to the left and Tucker was left wondering what the hell he'd been thinking, offering to let Kady sleep in his office.

It was just for a few hours.

Then it would be one more day down.

And not many to go.

Tucker had no idea how he felt about that. Neither was he going to try to figure it out.

He was just going to put his head down and keep moving. Until Kady finally caught her flight back to Atlanta.

CHAPTER FIVE

KADY DOG-PADDLED AROUND CONSCIOUSNESS, going past it a few times before circling back to find it.

Where was she?

Even when she opened her eyes, the darkness remained. She'd been sleeping, but this wasn't her hotel room, since her cheek was against something that was like leather, only cushier.

If not the hotel, then where?

She allowed her senses to drift, snuggling a little further under the thin blanket or whatever was on top of her.

Wait. She'd been at the hospital. Was supposed to check on someone.

A patient!

This time she sat up, struggling to see.

"It's okay. It's not midnight yet."

Low earthy tones drifted across the space as her eyes tried to adjust—as objects began materializing through the gloom. A desk. A chair. The shape of a person.

Tucker.

How long had she been asleep? From her groggy,

cotton-stuffed head, she was going to say it was only a couple of hours.

Had he been sitting in that chair the whole time, watching her?

The thought unnerved her. "What time is it?"

"Eleven thirty. I was going to wake you up in fifteen more minutes."

"I'm awake. Did you get any sleep?"

"Not yet."

Well, now she felt horrible. He had to be as exhausted as she was. They could have taken turns. Kady was used to getting in power naps when things were busy at the hospital in Atlanta. And the cots in the doctors' rest area weren't nearly as comfortable as this couch was. Which was probably why she'd slept so long.

Or maybe it was the way his scent clung to everything in the room, including the throw pillow.

Damn. Not a good thing to be thinking about when the room's occupant was just a few yards away.

He clicked on the light, and what she saw made her breath catch in her chest. Not because he looked atrocious. Tucker could never look anything other than gorgeous. But right now that attractive face was shadowed by a haggardness that made her heart ache. He looked like he'd gone to war and come out on the losing end. Well, he had been through a battle. They both had. And there was nothing she could do to make it better. That was what hurt the most. Her husband had ducked out of her life back then, and no amount of begging or pleading had brought him back.

"Sorry. You should have woken me up. Why don't

I take the chair for a while? Or, better yet, you could go home, if you wanted to."

"I have to scrub for surgery in a few hours."

"And you've had no sleep?" Anger zipped up her spine, more at herself than him. "You needed the rest more than I did."

"I said I didn't sleep. But I did rest. I've done this before. And it's not a complicated surgery."

Was there really any uncomplicated fetal surgery? From her perspective, no. But maybe there were degrees of difficulty in his field the same way her high-risk pregnancy field had different levels. Preeclampsia was different from full-blown eclampsia.

"What type of surgery?"

"The fetus has a diaphragmatic hernia."

Uncomplicated?

She didn't think so. A diaphragmatic hernia meant that a hole in the diaphragm was allowing abdominal organs to move into the chest cavity. Mortality rates could be high. "How bad is it?"

"It's one of the better cases I've seen. The heart and lungs are displaced, but the hole isn't large enough to allow widespread movement between the chest and the abdomen. If I can stretch an abdominal muscle over the spot as a kind of patch, it should help everything to stay put."

"What about the heart and lungs?"

"They should move back into place on their own. The patient is at twenty-nine weeks, so if we can keep her from going into labor right away, things should have a chance to right themselves before Tony is born."

"Tony?"

One side of his mouth quirked as if he'd been caught doing something he shouldn't. "It's the name they've chosen for the baby."

He'd cared enough to learn the baby's name?

Oh, God. A truckload of memories careened her way: Tucker speaking to her abdomen when she'd been carrying Grace. Tucker saying the baby's name over and over, believing she would hear it and have a sense of identity from the moment she was born.

He'd been right. She had seemed to know her name, eyes flickering with what could have been recognition soon after birth. Did he even remember?

"You used to talk to Grace before she was born, remember?"

He leaned back in his chair. "I do."

Not the most elaborate response, but at least he hadn't shut her down. She wished they could have sat and shared what they'd each loved most about their daughter, but they'd been too busy fighting each other to sit down and remember the good times.

"Do you talk to your patients while you operate?"

She could very easily imagine him doing that, telling them to hang in there, that he was going to try to fix whatever was wrong with their tiny bodies.

"The sedation we use for the mothers carries over to the babies, so they can't hear me." He paused for several long seconds. "But, yes. I talk to them."

She'd watched him operate before, cradling those tiny forms in his hands, moving with such care.

And he talked to them. The way he'd talked to Grace.

A rush of strong emotion welled up inside her,

blinding her for an instant. She took a deep breath and let it out in a long silent stream, trying not to examine her feelings too closely, afraid of what she might find lurking there.

She stood, dropping the blanket onto the sofa, and went around to the other side of the desk. "I'm so glad."

"Glad about what?"

A strange hoarseness had invaded his voice.

"That you talk to them."

Before she realized what was happening, he'd wrapped an arm around her waist and dragged her onto his lap. Then his mouth was on hers. And her world exploded. He hadn't wanted to touch her in a very long time, so to have him kissing her as if he couldn't get enough was heady. And terrifying.

Right now, she didn't care about patient charts or medical conferences or anything else.

A kaleidoscope of memories sent her reeling back through time, bits and pieces of the torn fabric of their old life sliding together to form something old but something totally different from what had been before.

The man who hadn't wanted to touch her, who'd shunned her embrace was suddenly not that man anymore. Instead, he was the person she'd known while they'd been dating, the husband who'd talked to his daughter through her stomach. The lover who'd shown her peaks she'd never known existed.

His lips turned hard and demanding in an instant, his tongue delving deep into her mouth as if he hadn't tasted her a thousand times over during their years together.

It was all new—all old.

One hand went to the back of her head, his fingers diving into her hair, his palm cradling her skull as he deepened the kiss even more. A sound erupted from the back of her throat. She tensed, afraid it would drive him away from her. It didn't. If anything, it pushed him closer.

He lifted her off his lap with a suddenness that left her reeling.

"What's wrong?"

"Nothing. Absolutely nothing."

He stood, scooping her up until she was cradled against his chest, and then he was moving toward the other side of the room.

Her mouth watered when she realized where he was going. All kinds of mental images flashed through her mind and she already knew that all of them would fall far short of what Tucker could make her feel. Was already making her feel.

He lowered himself to the cushion of the couch, still holding her tight. Her mouth found his again, and the kiss deepened, his tongue seeking entrance.

Yes!

She welcomed him in, the fiery sensation so familiar that an ache settled in her chest. But only for a minute.

Tucker's hands went to her waist, urging her to face him, mouths coming unlocked for a second or two as she scrambled to find a way to do what he wanted. Then she had a knee on either side of his thighs. And the second she lowered herself onto his lap, she knew it was over. This night was not going to end the way she'd expected it to when she came through the door to that office.

What did it matter? Because in this moment in time there was absolutely no place she would rather be than in his arms.

CHAPTER SIX

IT HAD BEEN so long. Too long. And the engine that couldn't all of a sudden could. And how.

It had roared to life with a suddenness that had sent his whole world spinning through space.

Why had it seemed so impossible before? He had no idea.

His hands went to her hips and shifted them down and forward, using the pressure to ease the ache that was forming in his groin. Only it didn't ease it. It made it jerk with a need that had him groaning for release.

"Damn." His hands went under her blouse, fingers scraping up the length of her spine before tangling in her hair. Those glorious, lustrous strands that had driven him crazy with need time after time. Oh, the things he'd done with them. With her.

Too many wants and needs to satisfy all at once. So he would start with this one.

The buttons on her blouse were calling him, so he undid one pearly bauble after another, revealing white lace beneath it all.

God.

Soft swells of pale flesh rose and fell with her breathing. And if she lowered herself onto him and pumped, that flesh would jiggle in a way that would drive him over the edge.

She was gorgeous. She always had been. But motherhood had added something that fit her to a T.

A squiggle of unease went through him.

No. Don't think about that. Not right now. A gentle tug on her hair had her neck arching back and soon his mouth was on her throat, sliding up to her ear, nipping the lobe. "Do you want this as much as I do?"

"Can't you tell?" The words rumbled against his skin, her breath warming his cheek.

"Not yet. Let's find out for sure. Stand up for a minute."

She blinked down at him, her confusion apparent, but she did as he asked, getting her legs under her, forcing him to let go of her hair. The lack of pressure against his zipper caused a pointed protest to go through him.

That was okay, because he had more important things to do right now. He undid the top of her slacks and slid the zipper down. Then he slid them down her hips and kept going until he reached her calves. Kady took it from there, kicking the garment off the rest of the way. But when she went to reach for her underwear, he stopped her, pulling her forward until she was standing on either side of his legs, her shins pressed against the front of the couch.

And he couldn't resist. Filling his hands with her ass, he held her still and pressed his face against the lower curve of her belly, feathering his lips across the silky underwear, making circles that gradually traveled lower and lower until…

A moan from somewhere overhead and hands that

were suddenly in his hair, holding tight, said he'd hit just the right spot. Her parted legs provided the perfect opportunity for his tongue to dip out and find a damp warmth.

"Mmm, yes, I think you do want this."

He should have let her take those panties off, but it was too late now. Besides, he was afraid he'd be tempted to finish things off too quickly. And the last thing he wanted right now was fast.

So he gently allowed his tongue to push forward and back, the increase in her breathing and tightening of fingers in his hair saying it was having the desired effect.

He loved driving her crazy. Always had.

It wasn't long before he was no longer satisfied with having the thin fabric between them. So he slid a finger beneath the elastic of her leg and eased it over. This time he was skin to skin and the first touch set up a pulsing in his groin that wasn't going to be denied.

"Tucker. Oh, God."

The sound of his name on her lips undid him. He didn't want slow any longer. One hand left her butt and moved to his fly, maneuvering until he'd freed himself. All he wanted to do was yank her down and feel that soft flesh slide over him, but he had to do something first.

He parted her. And kissed her. Right where he knew it counted. Right where experience had told him she liked it.

His lips closed around that tiny nub of flesh and sucked. Licked. Pulsed against it with rhythmic intent. Suddenly she was frantically pumping, ragged breaths telling him she was almost. Almost. *Almost.*

There!

He felt it the second she went off, and he wrapped an arm around the backs of her thighs, forcing her onto the couch. She was in as much of a hurry as he was, evidently, because she fought against his pull, scooting forward until she was above him, hands on his shoulders, eyes closed. She hesitated for the slightest second.

"Do it. *Hell*. Do it, Kady."

Then she was pushing down, encasing his aching flesh in a tight velvety space. Dammit. She was still pulsing, the sensations ripping right through any remnants of control he might have had. In an instant he was thrusting up into her, a massive surge of energy propelling him at a frantic rate. He erupted hard, the muscles in his legs turning to rock as his hands forced her down as far as she would go, his mind blanking out everything except the fierce waves of pleasure. Waves he never wanted to end. Hoped would go one and on and on.

Little by little, they subsided, his muscles starting to uncoil. His strokes slowed until her bottom was resting on his thighs. He tipped her against his chest as he leaned back against the sofa cushions behind him. His eyes had long since closed, and he had no desire to open them again. Except things were still happening. The rational side of his brain, which had been idling along in the background, began to move forward, a million questions starting to swirl and form actual thoughts.

What had just happened?

When could it happen again?

And how was he going to talk her into it?

Um, he was not going to talk anyone into anything.

He wasn't the only one who was starting to come to the conclusion that something enormous had just taken place. Kady shifted against him. He realized that he hadn't even gotten undressed. And Kady was barely undressed, her underwear pulled to the side, her bra still fastened in front.

And he'd forgotten to watch them jiggle.

That thought made him smile. He hadn't been in any condition to watch anything. He'd been on a fast track to disaster.

No. It wasn't a disaster.

Was it?

Oh, hell. Maybe it was.

Before he could ease her away from him, she sat up, her hands propelling her up and off his lap with a suddenness that made him grunt.

"Sorry," she said.

She didn't look sorry. And he wasn't sure if he should be apologizing or what. His head was still fuzzy and his mouth felt like it had been sucked dry by a vacuum. And he didn't know what the hell he was supposed to say. Or feel.

Her fingers hurried to her shirt and yanked it closed around her, buttons going back into their holes. Something was wrong.

Well, yeah, that was pretty obvious.

No. Not that.

Something was going on that was different than simply having sex.

Did she still have feelings for him?

His chest stuttered with something he could have sworn was fear.

What the hell had he been thinking?

By the time she'd yanked her slacks on, he'd decided he was definitely going to issue an apology. A big one. One that would cover any number of wrongs.

Before he got a chance, though, she scrubbed her hand up and down her other arm and took a deep breath. "I have something important I need to ask you."

No. She wasn't going to talk about feelings, was she? He was in no shape to try to stop and dissect what they'd just done. Not with his legs still shaking, and his head still trying to figure out where it was. Or how he'd let any of this happen.

It was just sex.

Right?

He forced the words out of his throat. "What is it?"

Dropping on to the couch next to him, she clasped her hands in her lap. "I'm not quite sure how to phrase this."

The feeling of impending doom that had been slowly circling overhead for the past three or four minutes darkened to storm cloud proportions. Irritation swept through his system, blotting out much of the pleasure he'd just experienced. "Just ask your question, Kady."

"Is there any chance I could get…? Um, did you…? Is there any way I can get pregnant from what we just did?"

He frowned, trying to form her words into something that made sense. "Pregnant."

His brain seized, sending bile washing up his throat when he realized what she was asking. She was wondering if he'd done what he'd been so determined not to do after Grace's death.

What in the name of everything holy was she implying?

Or maybe it wasn't what she was implying. Maybe the whole encounter had been planned, hoping to get around his refusals and get what she wanted.

No. Kady wouldn't do that. It was one thing he could state with all certainty. She didn't operate by subterfuge. If she wanted something, she asked.

At least the Kady he'd known before had. And this new, independent Kady? Was that how she operated as well? Did she think that if she somehow got pregnant, she could force them back together?

She'd given no indication that she was interested in him that way anymore. Until that kiss.

But...pregnant?

He was going to shoot down any tiny fragment of hope before it could form. In either of them.

"I had a vasectomy. I told you I was going to." He zipped himself back in. "So no. There's no chance. I've had follow-up exams just to make sure."

Her brows puckered. "Did you really hate being a father that much?"

"No, I hated losing a daughter that much."

And I hated not being able to make love to her mother afterward.

The fear of another pregnancy had paralyzed him. Obviously the surgery had fixed whatever had been broken.

No. It hadn't. It had simply fixed the symptom of that broken part of him. Yes, he could function again—and hell if it hadn't felt great—but the second she'd said the word *pregnant*, his heart had frozen into a block of ice that nothing could reach.

"I lost a daughter too, Tucker."

He got to his feet. "I realize that. Did you come to New York with an agenda?"

"What? No, of course not." The area between her brows puckered in anger. "How can you even say that? I never expected tonight to happen."

"Sorry." He dragged a hand through his hair. "This whole idea of pregnancy came on awfully quick. It never even crossed my mind."

She gave a dry laugh. "Maybe because *you* knew it was impossible. But I certainly didn't. And I needed make sure that if I *did* get pregnant anytime soon, I would know with certainty you aren't the father."

If she…

"How the hell would you get pregnant?"

Up went a brow.

"Let me rephrase that. Who would you be getting pregnant with?" If she said she had a boyfriend, he was going to punch a hole through the nearest flat object.

She crossed her arms under her breasts. "That's none of your business."

Anger threaded through his innards. "Lady, you just asked me if there was any possibility I was going to father a child with you. I think I have a right to know why."

Kady moved behind his desk, maybe needing to put some space between them. Well, she needn't have bothered, because right now there was an emotional gulf the size of a couple of universes between them.

"Fine, you want to know? I'm looking for a sperm donor."

A couple more layers of ice coated his chest wall. "And you thought I might be willing to oblige? Only you forgot one tiny detail. To ask permission."

Up went her chin. "I never needed your permission, because you were the last person I would have asked. I didn't mean for any of this to happen." Her hand swept toward the couch.

He couldn't stop the obvious question. "So who *were* you planning to ask?"

"No one. I've gone to a sperm bank. I'm in the process of selecting the best match."

The thought of Kady carrying someone else's baby made him feel physically ill. But he was the one who'd told her no over and over again. Not that he would have been able to get her pregnant back then.

"You're going to do artificial insemination?"

She shrugged. "I'm going to start there, and if that doesn't take, I'll try in vitro."

"You really do want another child, don't you?" His anger disappeared in an instant and regret took its place. Regret that he hadn't been able to give her what she needed. Regret that she'd needed it so badly that she hadn't been able to see past it.

"I told you I did." Her eyes turned sad. "Many times."

"I know. And I'm sorry it couldn't be me."

"It's over and done with. We're moving on." Her gaze went past him.

Was she talking about what had just happened between them? Yes, that was over and done with. But as far as moving on went? He was pretty sure the aftershocks of that encounter were going to be wreaking havoc with his system for a long time to come.

"So where do we go from here?"

Her head tilted, the confusion on her face plain. "What do you mean? *We* don't go anywhere from here. We decided that two years ago when we got a divorce. You go back to your life, and I'll go back to mine as soon as this conference is over."

"Of course." He wasn't even sure why he'd asked that question. It was better to bury any weird sentimental notions before they could take root and fester below the surface. "I phrased that badly. I meant how do we put what just happened behind us so we can finish out the rest of the seminar without it becoming awkward?"

This time she laughed, but there was no humor in the sound. "I think it became awkward the moment I landed in New York and realized you were at the conference. Wouldn't you agree?"

"No doubt about that." And yet they'd had sex.

"Are you going to be able to get past this?"

Said as if the only one she had doubts about was him. He was going to blow that idea out of the water. "I already am."

A skitter of some strong emotion passed through her eyes and then was gone replaced with a wary nod. "Me too. So we have nothing to worry about, then."

"No, nothing."

But deep in Tucker's heart he knew he just told the biggest lie of the century. Because the word *worried* didn't begin to cover the thoughts that were currently ricocheting through his head and threatening to explode into something far worse. It wasn't worry. Or concern. Or uneasiness.

This was more like the heavy dread that came with

knowing something big was just on the horizon. Something that would rock his world and change it forever. And no matter how hard he tried, he knew there was probably nothing he could do to stop it.

Tony's surgery was underway.

Kady had asked to observe, something about the case pulling at her.

Obviously…since it was what had sent her into his arms in the first place. Hearing him call that baby by name had touched a part of her she'd thought was dead. It wasn't.

And now that she was here, she was having trouble thinking about anything other than what had happened in Tucker's office. They hadn't even locked the door.

Anyone could have walked in.

The janitor. A patient. Even the department head.

Her stomach twisted.

At midnight? Not very likely. Even if anyone had known Tucker was in his office, they would have thought he was getting some much-needed sleep before the surgery.

And he had. At least she thought he had. After they kind of hashed out a tentative agreement for how to proceed professionally, he had stretched out on the couch again. But this time Kady hadn't stuck around. She'd told him she was going up to check on her patient and would be back before his surgery. She had peeked in on Samantha, but the young woman, of course, had been sound asleep. So Kady had gone down to the waiting room and curled up in one of the most uncomfortable chairs known to man and waited for the hour hand on the clock to creep around to five o'clock.

Then she'd met Tucker back at his office. When she'd arrived, he had already showered and dressed. He offered her the use of the tiny cubicle in his bathroom, which she gladly accepted. But even his shower carried his clean masculine scent, a stark reminder of what they had done hours earlier. Once his surgery was over, she was going straight to her own hotel room and rid herself of any trace of it.

At least she hoped she could.

She glanced down at the operating-room floor again, and every thought suddenly vanished when Tucker lifted something, his lips moving as he said something to someone…

Yes, I talk to them.

She swallowed hard. He was talking to the baby he held in his hands.

Tony.

Her ex bent low over the tiny form, his big body now blocking her view. But she'd seen it. It was unbelievable that surgery could be done on a fetus that size. But she'd watched Tucker operate more than once during their marriage, so why was it so surprising to see him do it now?

Maybe because she couldn't reconcile the Tucker who under no circumstances wanted another child—who had gone so far as to guarantee it would never happen—with the Tucker who could take a baby from its temporary home and treat it with such tender care. To repair the little one so that it had the best possible chance of living and thriving once it entered the real world.

Which man was the real Tucker Stevenson?

Maybe he was both. Or neither. Maybe the true man was somewhere in between.

He was still young. The fact that he'd made such a permanent decision about his fertility should tell her how strongly he'd felt about the whole thing. When they had been together she'd thought his reluctance was a result of his grief and that with time he would work through it and come round. That hadn't been the case.

Just then he glanced up at the observation window, causing her thoughts to freeze. It only lasted a second or two, but even that brief look made a shiver go through her. How was she going to get through the rest of the day, much less the rest of the week?

They were set to meet the medical students for rounds almost immediately after this surgery and then they had the conference later this afternoon.

He took a step to the side, glancing up at her again.

Why was he…?

He was trying to make sure she could see. That gesture made her heart squeeze. No matter how often she'd tried to cast him in the role of bad guy, he proved her wrong time and time again: sending flowers to Grace's grave; the funny tone he'd had when asking her who she was getting pregnant with; the way he'd just taken a few steps to the left.

The way he'd made love to her?

No, that had been sex.

Just sex.

Are you sure?

Oh, Lord, she'd better hope so. For her heart's sake.

Because even if it meant something more to her, there was no future in it.

And Kady was not willing to have a meaningless fling. Even with her ex-husband.

Tucker's low voice came over the speaker, detailing each step of the procedure just as he'd done the entire time. He was steady. Steady hands. Steady voice. Steady presence.

At least he had been.

"Kady, do you have any questions up there, before I close up shop?"

Questions? Oh, she had plenty. But none of them were about Tony. Or the procedure.

But now every head in the surgical suite had swiveled toward her, probably wondering how Tucker knew her or, worse, if they were dating.

Ha! They hadn't dated in a very long time. And when they had…

Think up something intelligent! Professional.

She leaned close to the tiny microphone hanging in front of her, glad her earlier thoughts hadn't been captured by it. "Will the surgery have to be redone in the future? Or will this procedure be the only repair needed?"

Tucker's eyes found hers and held them. "We can hope this will be it. But there are never any guarantees."

Just like she'd hoped that their divorce would bring an end to all the heartache she'd endured. But it never quite went away. She'd had opportunities to date over the last couple of years, but she just hadn't had the energy or desire to start over.

Maybe that's what looking for a sperm donor was

all about. A new start. A chance to finally make that break with the past.

Except, even in death, Grace would always be a point of connection. Like the fresh flowers she found whenever she went to visit her daughter's grave.

"Well, I hope for his sake that he can go on from here without ever needing to think about what happened today."

And if that didn't sound like wishful thinking, she didn't know what did. Because she would never be able to get away from thinking about what had happened in his office last night.

"That's the hope. Okay, let's get this little guy back where he belongs. Good job, everyone."

With one last glance up at where she was sitting, Tucker bent over his patient once again and began closing up the gaping wounds his scalpel had created.

If only they could each find someone who could do the same for them.

Whoever had said time healed all wounds had either been crazy or a damned liar.

Because looking at Tucker still hurt.

And she had no idea when that ache would finally go away.

CHAPTER SEVEN

HE'D HOPED THE conference would be a refuge.

No such luck. He and Kady had been thrust once again into the same workshop after a disastrous day following an even more disastrous night. The medical students who'd followed them around had had questions. Lots of them. Some of them having to do with colleague relationships. Platonic ones, but it still made Kady's face light up like a neon sign.

Afterward, they'd had to rush over to the conference center together. This was the seminar he'd been dreading the most: Genetics and Pregnancy—identifying common abnormalities. And, of course, Kady was the replacement for Dr. Blacke so she was there with him. Seated next to him this time. Colleague relationships indeed.

If he'd known, he might have feigned a patient emergency and risked the wrath of Phil Harold if someone checked up on his excuse.

But since they'd come together, Kady would have known immediately why he was skipping out on the session.

He glanced over at her. Nothing was in front of her. No notes. No computer tablet. Well, that made two of them. He had no intention of saying a word other than his short canned speech, unless one of the audience members asked him something point blank.

Like about interdepartmental relationships?

Why would anyone ask something like that? He was imagining things that weren't there.

Or were they?

Dammit, Tucker, knock it off!

The microphone passed to the third panel member, who, according to his bio, was a researcher in the area of bioengineering. "Okay, so true story—I went to college to get a degree in music. I wanted to be a concert pianist. I had it all going for me—hard work and a drive to succeed. And then... I met a girl." He paused when knowing laughter erupted across the audience.

"Well, things got serious, and she got pregnant. We got married, and we both continued going to school. She went into labor five weeks early. We were scared but unbelievably happy. And then our life together changed forever. Our boy—Alexander—was born a harlequin baby. He never came home from the hospital."

He swallowed hard.

Harlequin ichthyosis was a terrible condition where thick scalelike armor encased a newborn's body. It created treatment challenges that were difficult if not impossible to overcome.

It was equally impossible not to notice the parallel threads that ran between the bioengineer's story and Tucker and Kady's saga.

Unexpected pregnancy. *Check.* Quick marriage. *Check.* Baby born with devastating fatal condition. *Check.*

Tucker couldn't even bring himself to glance at Kady to see if she was thinking the same thing he was.

"In a matter of months, I changed my major from music to medicine, studying how genetics affect the human story. It was the only way I could think of to make sense of my son's death."

Was there a way to make sense of a thing like that?

Maybe each person dealt with tragedy differently. Tucker peered sideways at the woman next to him. Kady's head was down, and she was staring at a closed manila folder to the right of her.

Yes. She was thinking of Grace too. Or at least he thought she was.

He couldn't stop his hand from covering hers.

When she glanced up at him, her eyes glistened, but that was the only sign that this topic was affecting her. Him? It was damn well ripping his heart from his chest.

She squeezed his fingers and then let him go, maybe afraid someone would see them and wonder what was going on.

He used to be weirdly fascinated with genetic abnormalities. Had been called in to consult on a number of them. Now he tried to avoid them whenever possible. So whatever had driven the researcher to abandon his goals and dive into the deep end of the very condition that had killed his child had passed Tucker over.

He'd never operated on a Tay-Sachs baby. It didn't normally show up until six months after birth. Or when routine testing revealed the lack of an enzyme needed to break down fatty material.

Tay-Sachs was a death sentence. Grace had slowly

lost her ability to do things, her motor skills decreasing at an alarming rate until she had been paralyzed.

And unlike the man who'd just laid his heart on the table for everyone to see, Tucker had no intention of mentioning Grace. Or anything else personal. That was his cross to bear.

When it was his turn to speak, he just rattled off a few obvious areas where genetics and fetal surgery overlapped. He then nodded to Kady, giving her the floor.

"Thank you, Dr. Stevenson. Almost every inherited condition that we are able to identify prenatally automatically changes that patient's status to high risk. Obviously we wish we could identify every anomaly before birth, but we just can't. The best option, if you know you carry a certain gene, is to get genetic counseling. *Before* getting pregnant, if possible." She paused and drew a deep breath. "But even if you find out about the condition *after* having a baby, I strongly urge you to get counseling. Not to is irresponsible."

By the time she finished, his abdominal muscles were rock-hard. Maybe she wasn't talking about him. But what else could she be referring to?

There'd been no need to get counseling, since they weren't going to have more children together. Ever.

Or maybe she had been talking about herself, since she was thinking of getting pregnant through a sperm donor. His gut tightened even further.

How the hell was she going to make sure her donor wasn't a carrier, unless the sperm bank tested everyone? Or maybe they did nowadays. He had no idea, because the thought of donating sperm made him sick.

By the time the Q & A portion of the seminar came

around, Tucker had a raging headache that started at the back of his neck and stretched like a band over the top. Maybe because he'd gotten less than five hours' sleep last night and had done surgery, led around a pack of medical students for most of the afternoon and now was here at the conference. A sixteen-hour day. And less than twenty-four hours since he and Kady had made love.

"Dr. McPherson, can you give us an idea of what types of cases you would refer for genetic counseling?"

There was a long pause while Kady waited for the microphone, which had moved further down the table. Her fingers were pressed tight against the laminated surface, but other than that telltale sign of nerves, there was no indication that the question bothered her.

The microphone landed in front of her.

She cleared her throat. "There are any number of inherited disorders that I've seen or worked with over the years. Sickle cell, thalassemia, hemophilia, some types of breast cancers, and Tay-Sachs are a few of them."

The words *Tay-Sachs* hit him like a hammer blow.

"Thank you. Can I ask one more question related to that?"

"Certainly." Her fingertips seemed to push harder against the table, turning white.

"Do you ever have patients who refuse genetic counseling? If so, would you refuse treat them if they were to become pregnant again?"

"I would never refuse to treat anyone." If anything, she sounded surprised by the question. "As for patients refusing testing, there are more of them than you might think."

Like Tucker?

She went on. "As for why, I think most of it boils down to fear. But what people should realize is that knowledge is a powerful tool."

And sometimes it wasn't. He'd pretty much read the whole encyclopedia when it came to his daughter's illness. He had a whole lot of head knowledge. But it changed nothing. Not then. And not now.

That person sat and another stood.

Hell, how long was this going to go on?

"This question is directed to the panel as a whole. If someone knew they had a recessive gene and it was unlikely that their significant other had the same gene, should they tell their partner?"

The harlequin baby's father motioned for the microphone. When it arrived, he looked the person straight in the eye. "Yes. Always. What Dr. McPherson said is true. If you know and don't tell, and your partner unknowingly carries that same gene, you could endanger any child you might have. Are you willing to take that risk?"

His vasectomy had kind of taken care of that. And now Kady knew about it.

Damn.

He'd let things go way too far last night.

His head told him he was a fool. His body told him he was a fool too. A lucky one. One who wanted more of what it had just gotten.

Not happening. Ever again.

As in never.

Three more days and the convention would be over.

Caput. In the history books. And his ex would be out of his life all over again.

It was only when people started getting up and bunching at the exit that he realized the workshop was over.

Kady turned to him. "I hope you didn't think I was directing any of that at you."

"Any of what?"

She frowned, making him revise his answer. "It doesn't matter who it was aimed at. It was good advice."

"Thanks. I had a patient a few months ago who was a carrier for sickle cell. She and the father were dating on and off, and she got pregnant. When the baby was born he had the condition. Unfortunately the couple was on the outs with each other and she refused to allow us to notify him."

"Wow. So he might not have even known he was a carrier."

"No." She sighed. "Think about what could happen if he fathers another child with a different woman and she finds out he already has a child with sickle cell."

"It wouldn't be his fault."

"No. But the child would pay the price."

"The first child paid the price anyway." Most people weren't tested unless they had a familial history.

"Maybe, but why let it be for nothing?"

A thought came to him. "Did you go through counseling? After Grace's death, I mean."

She swiveled her chair to look at him. "I did. I found out there are options."

"Such as?"

"Like having any potential sperm donor tested for

the mutation. Or fertilizing a couple of my eggs and having them tested for Tay-Sachs before they're implanted."

It all sounded logical when you looked at it with the objective lens of science. It was obvious she'd given this a lot of thought. Had done her research. But didn't she know that it wasn't just Tay-Sachs that was a danger? Anything could happen to that future fetus. A rogue mutation. A glitch during implantation. During the first trimester.

And she was willing to risk losing another child? The thought of a second gravestone next to Grace's was eerie. Lightning couldn't strike twice, right?

It could with them.

"Does having a baby mean that much to you that you're willing to risk it?"

"It does." Her eyes sought his. "I'm sorry that's something you never understood."

"I understood." He just hadn't agreed with her. As much as he'd wished he could have given her what she wanted, neither his head nor his body would cooperate. It was why he'd been so willing to let her go. To let her find what she needed elsewhere. He was only surprised that it had taken her this long to go through with it.

Someone clearing their throat made him glance up sharply. He was surprised to find a young woman standing in front of them, the snug waistline of her dress showing off what was obviously a pregnancy. Third trimester, if he wasn't mistaken.

He had no idea how much of their conversation she'd heard. Kady must have been wondering the same thing because her face was stiff and wooden-looking. "Can I help you?" he asked.

The woman nodded, her dark hair sliding forward to cover part of her face. "Did you mean what you said?"

The question was directed at Kady.

"About what?"

"About informing partners of your genetic history." The softness of her voice gave her away.

"Absolutely." Kady's head tilted. "Why do you ask?"

"My mom recently found out that she has breast cancer. She's turning fifty this year. She has the BRCA 1 mutation." Her hands twisted under her belly. "I was tested a couple of months ago. I have it too. What if my baby...? It's a girl."

Kady stood to her feet. "Just because you have the mutation it doesn't mean you'll get cancer. Or that your baby will develop it."

"What if I pass the gene on to my daughter? Can she be tested?"

That was a tricky question. And it was in a gray area as far as ethics went. "My gut reaction is no. There are no preventative guidelines in place for children."

"So she just has to wait?"

"Most health professionals I know would say yes. Is there a partner in the picture? If so, what does he or she say?"

"Her father—my husband—doesn't know yet."

Kady went to the edge of the dais and sat on it, putting her a little closer to the young woman. "Tell him. He has a right to know."

"That I might pass a terrible disease on to our baby? How does that help anyone?"

"You two are in this together. That means trusting each other with sensitive information." She glanced over at Tucker.

"I know you're right. But what if he leaves me?" The words were barely above a whisper.

Hell. That was always a possibility. Tucker had left, hadn't he? But only so she could have the freedom she needed to go after what she wanted in life.

"Wilson-Ross has a genetic counselor on staff. Why don't you go and talk to them? They can help you come up with a plan."

The woman drew a deep breath, whether in relief or resignation he wasn't sure. "Do you think they can?"

"That's what they're there for. Do it, if only for your own peace of mind." She smiled. "And give that husband of yours a chance to do the right thing. He might surprise you."

Kady had given Tucker the same chance by asking him to go to counseling with her and he'd refused.

Would counseling have changed his mind? He didn't think so. But she'd asked him to go. Had looked into his eyes and forced him to make a choice. He had. It just hadn't been the one she'd been hoping for.

Had he done the right thing? He'd thought so at the time but he was beginning to wonder.

"Thank you." Her soft words were directed at both of them, even though he hadn't said a thing. Hadn't been able to think of one helpful comment.

And yet Kady had known just the right thing to say.

"Tucker, can you hand me a pen and a piece of paper, please?"

Frowning, he tore off the back cover of the booklet for the workshop and handed it to her, along with one of the monogrammed pens that Wilson-Ross had given them.

Kady scribbled something and handed it to the woman. "This is the hospital's main number. Call them. Tell them you need to speak with a genetic counselor. Let them help you, like they did me."

"You act like you have the gene or something."

"Let's just say it's the 'or something.' My daughter was born with an incurable, inherited gene. She died when she was two years old."

"I'm so sorry."

"It was the hardest thing I've ever gone through. Do I wish she'd never been born? No. Not for a second. So I think I might understand a little more than most people what it's like to receive a piece of devastating news."

"How did the father take it?"

Without skipping a beat, she said, "We're no longer together. But it doesn't have to be that way for you. Talk to a counselor, and then talk to your husband."

It was like taking a stomach punch to the gut. Was she saying she could have done something that would have given their marriage a different outcome? He didn't see how.

"Okay, I will. And I'm sorry your husband didn't think your relationship was worth fighting for."

Not worth fighting for? Hell, he'd fought for her with all he'd been worth. None of it had been enough to change her mind. And she hadn't been able to change his. Their marriage had been as doomed as his daughter.

As the young woman walked away, Kady turned to him. "I don't think that, you know."

He shrugged. This wasn't something he wanted to talk about over a cup of coffee or anything else. In fact, he'd rather they not discuss it at all. Especially not after the day he'd had.

"It's okay. She obviously didn't overhear as much of our conversation as I thought she did." He picked up his packet of notes. Notes he hadn't needed after all. "Do you want me to give you a ride back to the hotel?"

"No, it's only a block away. I think I'll walk. I need the exercise."

Or did she just not want to be stuck in a car with him?

"You sure?"

"Yes. I could use some fresh air. See you in the morning."

And he could use some time alone to get his head back together. Somehow being with this woman made him crazy. And brought back feelings both good and bad, that he hadn't felt since he'd left Atlanta.

A sense of foreboding stole over him. He'd thought his life would go back to normal in three more days. Once she got on that plane and headed out.

The door to the conference center closed, leaving him standing in an empty room. Would life really go back to normal? Or would he just realize how alone he really was? In more ways than one.

CHAPTER EIGHT

KADY'S PHONE WAS RINGING. She could hear it through the door to the shower, but with suds in her hair and an ache in her heart she decided to just let her voice mail pick it up. She wasn't in Atlanta, so it wasn't her hospital calling with an emergency regarding one of her patients.

Tilting her head back to let the sharp spray power-wash the shampoo from her wet locks, she tried to clear her head. Something that no amount of fresh air had been able to do last night.

She still had an hour before she was supposed to be back at the hospital for another round of medical students. God, how was she supposed to face Tucker again after yesterday? She didn't have any choice, unless she went home early. A tantalizing thought, but not something she was going to do. People had to face exes all the time in the real world. She just needed to suck it up and deal with it.

Most people didn't wind up sleeping with those exes, though.

Well, that had been a one-time thing. It wasn't like they were going to hook up every night while she was here. A tingle stole across her belly and slid lower, following the trail of water from the shower.

"Not happening," she told it. "Forget it."

As if forgetting it was an option. If Tucker was anything, he was a great lover. Except for those last horrible months of their marriage when he hadn't been able to stand the sight of her naked. When every touch from her had been met with a cold shoulder and an even colder heart.

And yet the night before, he'd kissed her as if he couldn't get enough. As if having sex with her was the only thing he could think of. Just like in the early days of their relationship.

That was what had done her in. What was still doing her in. What had changed in the two years since they'd seen each other? He'd gone from cold to very, *very* hot.

Whatever it was, she wanted nothing to do with it. Maybe she should say that out loud, just in case.

"You want nothing to do with it. Nothing to do with him."

Ha. Well, that did a whole lot of nothing, because that tingle spread to an uncomfortable level. Finishing her shower in a hurry, she dried off then wrapped the oversize towel around her hair and padded into the bedroom to check her phone. The missed call was an Atlanta number she didn't recognize. Maybe it was about a patient after all.

Sitting on the mattress, she pushed the button to return the call, adjusting the towel so she could get the phone to her ear.

"Atlanta Fertility Services, may I help you?"

Her heart skipped a beat. This was the firm she'd

contacted about finding a sperm donor for her. She still had the envelope from them in her purse, as far as she knew. She just hadn't planned on contacting them again until she got back to town.

"This is Dr. Kadeline McPherson. I had a missed call from this number."

"Oh, yes, Dr. McPherson. Dr. Torres would like to speak to you personally. Can you hold for a moment?"

"Yes."

The soft sounds of a vaguely familiar melody drifted across the line. Why was the fertility clinic calling her? Of course they didn't realize she was in New York. It had never dawned on her to tell them. Maybe they'd found something in her application that needed to be redone.

Her heart stuttered. Or maybe they'd found something else in her lab work. Another genetic anomaly that would knock her out of the running for ever having a child.

No. She'd run a gamut of tests when she'd gone through genetic counseling. She had the Tay-Sachs gene but nothing else had turned up. At least, nothing known.

The music cut off. "Dr. McPherson?"

"Yes."

"I wanted to check in. We've identified several donors who would be excellent prospects. Tay-Sachs testing is negative, along with any other known genetic factors. Do you want to come in and look at the files?"

Her stomach squirmed and she had no idea why. She'd been excited to move on to this next phase in her life a few short weeks ago.

Before she'd come to New York?

No, that had nothing to do with it. She was just nervous. This was a huge step. "I'm actually out of town at the moment. Would you be able email the files to me, so I can take a look?"

"That's not a problem. Our front desk should have your email address, correct?"

"It was on my paperwork."

There was a pause. "Is everything okay?"

No, but she wasn't sure why. "Yes, it's just hectic here. I'm at a medical conference."

He chuckled. "I understand. I've been to a few of those myself."

"You know what I'm talking about, then." Her words sounded stilted even to her. "But I should be home in a few more days. I can look them over and let you know my thoughts. Is that okay?"

"Perfect. I'll let Jessica up front know. You should get the files sometime today."

"Thank you."

"You're welcome. If you have any other questions, just give us a call."

She ended the call, a chill washing over her. Was it her imagination or did Dr. Torres sound a little more eager than he had when she'd originally met with him? She groaned and dropped her phone onto the bed. It was her imagination. He didn't sound any different now than he had a month ago. Maybe it was her who had changed.

Seeing Tucker again had turned her world on its head. Everything seemed upside down and inside out—a place where the words *simple* and *uncomplicated* no longer existed. But they would. Once she got home.

The phone rang again. "Surely not."

She picked it up and pressed the green button. "Hello?"

"Kady? Where are you?"

This time, it was Tucker's voice that came over the line. Her heart thudded and it took a couple of swallows before she could speak. "I'm sorry?"

"Didn't you get my message?"

"What message?"

"I called you about ten minutes ago. Your patient is asking for you." She'd given him her cellphone number after she'd left his office that fateful night. At the time she told herself it was to make reaching her a little easier in case of a schedule change.

Pulling the phone away from her ear, she looked at the time. It was just eight o'clock. She wasn't supposed to be at the hospital for another hour. "My patient?"

Wow, she sounded like an idiot responding to everything with a question. But Tucker put her head in a spin every time she heard his voice…felt his touch. Like the moment he'd unsnapped the button on her pants and…

No more touching. No more kissing. No more anything except work. Hadn't she just had this talk with herself a few minutes ago?

"Your patient from the birthing center."

The name and face came to her in an instant. "Samantha? The PPH patient?"

"Yes, she's leaving today and wants to see you."

The chill from a few moments ago disappeared. "Did someone get a hold of her roommate?"

"I think she's on her way to pick her up."

"Tell her I'll be there in fifteen minutes." The medical students would have to forgive her wet hair and lack of makeup. Some things were just more important.

Like having a baby of her own?

Maybe.

True to her word, she arrived in fifteen minutes. And she'd obviously just showered not long ago. Her hair was twisted up in one of those clawed contraptions that she used to wear at home all the time.

If he undid it and let those silky strands tumble down her back, he knew just what scent would cling to them. Vanilla, coconut…and Kady. He forced the air in his nostrils to exit, hoping to avoid searching for any hint of it. He'd been knocked on his ass last night during her conversation with that young woman. It seemed everywhere he'd turned recently, something had done just that. Making him rethink decisions he'd once thought were irrevocable. Like having children?

Kind of hard to do that with a vasectomy.

"Is she still here?"

"She's waiting for you in her room. Four forty-one."

"No more problems?"

He shook his head, forcing his gaze from her wet hair to her face. It looked fresh scrubbed as well, her pale lashes bereft of mascara, the smattering of freckles across her nose on full display. More memories crowded into his skull, each less welcome than the one before. And there wasn't a damn thing he could do about it. "They wouldn't release her if they thought there was."

"Thank you for calling me."

"I tried to let you off the hook, but she insisted."

"I was planning on checking on her this morning. I didn't realize they were going to discharge her already. I'm used to making those kinds of decisions, but I guess she wasn't really mine."

"Yes, she was. You pulled her through that crisis."

"I'm glad I was here."

She put a hand to her hair, as if checking to make sure it was still secured, then went back to worrying at that empty ring finger. He hated that it was bare, hated that she kept drawing his attention to it.

She stopped fiddling and looked at him. "I'm glad you were there too."

"Are you?" A clod of something stuck in his throat, making his voice come out rougher-sounding than it should have.

"You did a lot to help keep her calm."

The wind went out of his sails in a hurry. Of course she hadn't meant she was glad in a more personal sense. He decided to change the subject.

"You didn't have to rush right over. I'm sure she would have waited for you."

"That bad, huh?"

He frowned. "I'm not sure what you mean."

"The way I look. I didn't put on any makeup."

Ah, that's what...

"I think I remember telling you I liked you without it. Many times."

"Patients always looked at me like I was a kid without it."

No one would mistake her for a kid anymore. Not because she looked older. Yes, there were tiny lines beside her eyes and a crease on the right side of her face where her smile reached slightly higher. The biggest change was in those green eyes. Eyes that had seen things no one should ever have to see. Had held her daughter in her arms as she'd taken her final breath.

She wasn't older. There were just moments he caught a fleeting sadness in her eyes. Or was that resignation?

He had no doubt the experience had aged him too. Only he hadn't handled it nearly as well as she had. Grace's death had nearly crippled him emotionally. He'd never been as open as Kady and her family were about showing their feelings. Their grief had been almost palpable—expressed the way healthy people were supposed to. Tucker, on the other hand, had built a dam, shoving his emotions behind it.

After everything had gone south, he'd retreated into himself with the lame excuse that he needed to be strong for his wife. In the end, she had been the one who'd been strong for him. She'd been able to function emotionally…sexually, even in the midst of her grief. And he hadn't been able to deal with that. So he'd shut her out. Along with her family and most of the world. When Kady's grandfather had tried to talk to him, he'd slammed that mental door as well.

For Tucker, shame and grief had gone hand in hand and created an unholy alliance. A wall had gone up that had never come down. It still hadn't.

"I can go home afterward and dry my hair at least."

Damn, she'd taken his lengthy silence for disapproval.

"Leave it. I like it."

As if that should matter one iota. He always managed to say the wrong thing around her.

"Okay, I will."

And with that simple answer and the smallest glimmer of a smile she started walking toward the room. She glanced back and tossed her head in a *come on* gesture. "You were in that treatment room as well."

"I don't think she even remembers me. It was you she wanted to see."

"Somehow I doubt that very many people forget you, Tucker. You kind of blow through like a hurricane."

He blinked. "Is that a compliment?"

"It's just the reality."

And leaving him to wonder what the hell she meant by that, she headed toward the room, leaving him to follow behind.

Once they got there they found someone already there, holding the baby. "Dr. McPherson, thanks so much for coming. This is my roommate, Phoebe."

"I'm glad I got to see you before you left." Kady's thumb went to town on her ring finger, like she should be doing something but wasn't sure what.

Ah, she wasn't used to being with a patient without checking vitals or doing something doctorly. He understood that all too well. It wasn't always easy to have relationships that weren't based on either professional courtesy or trying to help patients. It was why doctors sometimes had a hard time switching off once the last patient had been seen. There were days there just wasn't anything left for anyone else. Not fair to families sometimes. Tucker had always thought he and Kady had had the perfect arrangement, because they'd understood that and had given each other space when it was needed.

But when the same two doctors couldn't fix what

was wrong with their daughter, that house of cards came tumbling down. Nothing known to man had been able to reconstruct it. Maybe he'd never have another real relationship ever again. And maybe it was even easier that way.

Was work enough?

It had been. At least until now. And once Kady went home? Would it be enough again?

He had no idea. But he sure as hell hoped so. When his eyes ventured to that black hair clip, though, all bets were off. Because the cycle of remembering and rejecting began all over again.

"Do you want to hold her?" Samantha's voice brought him back from the brink, and he realized she was talking to him. At some point the baby had passed from Samantha's roommate to Kady.

She was standing with the newborn tucked into her arms, gently rocking the infant back and forth. Nothing had ever looked more right than seeing her with a baby. His breath stalled in his throat, even as he noted her eyes on him, a worried crease between her brows. Had Samantha already asked him once?

"Oh, no. I'm good."

"Aw, come on," the young woman coaxed. "I know you know how to hold a baby. You operate on ones smaller than this one all the time, right? At least, that's what Dr. McPherson told me. How about holding one that's healthy?"

Healthy.

Had Kady told her about Grace?

No. They were talking in generalities. And if he refused to hold the newborn, someone was going to wonder why.

The breath he'd been holding in stagnated in his lungs and his throat tightened. Somehow, though, he managed to hold his arms out when Kady came over, allowing her to gently deposit the tiny bundle into his care.

No one should ever trust him with a baby.

And yet patients did it every day.

This was different, though. This baby had weight. And substance. And…health.

What he was feeling now was probably the same thing Kady had felt a few moments ago.

Grace had felt just like this once upon a time. Just a day old, but with a solidness that had felt very right in his arms. Smoky blue had eyes met his and blinked. Blond tufts of hair had stood straight up. Small fists had waved in the air as if…

He couldn't do it. "Take her, please." He held the baby out for Kady to take back, while chunks of his heart seemed to peel away and fall to the floor.

How could she bear the thought of having another child? Holding it close? Loving it?

He could treat preterm babies because he knew they weren't his. And it was his way of doing what he hadn't been able to do for Grace: give them a cure. But there was no attachment. No sentimental feelings attached to any of them. He made sure of that.

Then why did their names run through his head as he operated on them? Why did he murmur to them, even as his scalpel cut deep?

He was just trying to remember that what he did was important to someone.

Samantha took the baby from Kady with a smile. "Thanks again for everything."

She acted like there was nothing weird about the way he'd rushed the infant back into Kady's arms. Maybe he hadn't been as transparent as he'd thought. Or maybe he was better at hiding his emotions than he gave himself credit for.

They walked the trio out to the curb, waiting while the baby was strapped into a car seat in the roommate's car. Then they waved goodbye.

This was the last time they would ever see Samantha and her new baby. He tried to drum up the last time he'd seen his own baby, but failed miserably.

"Tucker, are you okay?"

Kady's soft voice called him back from the depths. "I'm fine. Just didn't expect to have to hold her, that's all."

"I could tell." She linked her arm through his for a moment as they stood there on the curb, the noise of traffic and voices outside very different from the canned silence inside the hospital. "You were a good father to her. Don't ever forget that."

A sudden wash of emotion spurted from behind the wall, stabbing at the backs of his eyes and clogging his throat. Oh, hell. Not now.

He pulled his arm from hers, afraid if they stood there any longer, she would see.

"We did everything we could for her. So did her doctors." His cool businesslike tone had to be a slap in the face after what she'd just said. But it was all he could manage without the past pouring out in a very real way.

She gripped his arm again. "Hey, don't do that. Don't you *dare* do that."

"Do what?"

"Act like she was nothing more to you than one of your patients. She was our *daughter*, dammit."

"You think I don't know that? That I don't have to deal with what happened every single hour of every single day?" The dam broke and he turned, yanking her against him. "I remember the second she was born, the second she smiled. The second she…"

Then his lips were on hers, hand going to the back of her head and clutching her to him. Grief and want and need all melded together into a huge tangled ball that was impossible to unravel.

Kady seemed to understand exactly what he was feeling, arms wrapping around his neck, giving back every bit as good as she got.

And it *was* good—too good—the heat and pressure of her mouth changing the tone in an instant. He deepened the kiss, and a familiar stirring took place, reminding him that he could indeed do things. *Wanted* to do them.

With Kady and no one else.

"Woohoo! Go, Dr. Stevenson!" The cheer, along with several catcalls, had him yanking away from her so fast that she tripped backward, might have fallen if he hadn't reached out to grab her arm.

Thirteen figures stood on the sidewalk, staring at them. Some of them grinning, some of them shocked as hell. Well, no one was more shocked than Tucker himself.

What did he do about it? This was his fault. He'd initiated that kiss. It was bad enough that the medical students had seen it. Who else had spotted them?

Great. How was he supposed to explain this to anyone?

Worse, how was he supposed to explain this to himself?

This was why he didn't let his emotional responses come out to play more often. They ran amok, doing whatever the hell they wanted to.

He took a breath.

"We just had a… This was…"

Kady took a step forward. "Remember when we talked about interpersonal relationships? This was a lesson in what not to do with a colleague. I hope you all got the point."

Whether they believed the hogwash she was dishing up or not, they didn't dare contradict her. While he willed his body to turn off the fireworks she'd unwittingly ignited, Kady was busy running over the latest case study with the group. A case he couldn't even remember going over with her.

Because he hadn't given her the chance. He'd whisked her back to that hospital room to see their patient and things had slalomed downhill from there.

Until that kiss, when things had started going up in ways they shouldn't have. But Tucker had proved one thing to himself.

He hadn't forgotten the smell of her hair.

Or her touch. Or anything else about her.

It was still there. In the back of his memory bank.

And there wasn't any power on earth that was going to erase it. Not three days from now, when she went home. Not three months from now. And probably not three hundred years from now.

CHAPTER NINE

KADY SAT BY the pool and tried to make out the words on the documents. Not easy on her phone. Making the text bigger helped, but then she had to scroll repeatedly back and forth to follow the sentences from beginning to end.

She should probably just wait until she got home to go over the sperm donors' information, but she'd wanted to give it a chance to percolate for a while.

Anything to take away the memory of that scene in front of the hospital. She'd been shocked by the outpouring of emotion from a man who hadn't let her see the real him in a very long time. She'd glimpsed it when he'd been so desperate to hand the baby back to her. But during that kiss? Lightning had cracked through the air, singeing them both. And something had woken inside her. Some vital part that had tunneled into the earth had sprung back to life, leaves unfurling and seeking the sun.

But if she'd hoped Tucker would declare that he'd never stopped loving her, that he'd changed his mind, she'd been sorely disappointed.

But, then, she'd been disappointed before.

She focused on the information on the screen.

It was all there. Height, weight, body type, ethnic background. The first two she rejected outright, although she wasn't quite sure why. They seemed perfect on paper. What wasn't to like? They were both evidently tall, dark and handsome. So what was wrong?

She had no idea.

Tipping her sunglasses to the top of her head, thinking maybe the artificial darkness was injecting some kind of pessimism into the process, she tried again. The glare from the white paper hurt her eyes. There was no foggy residue on the windows today to mute the sunlight. She squinted and forced her eyes to keep moving, trying to pinpoint the problem.

She found nothing.

Why was she having such a hard time differentiating between one application and the next? Maybe it was having the sanitized, clinical reality laid out in front of her. This was not a love match. Or computer dating. Then again, it wasn't meant to be. It was scientific data, nothing more, nothing less.

But taking the human element away made it seem like all three applicants were painted with the same brush. No mention of a dimple. No stray acne scar on any of their right temples. No crooked little toe from a break when he'd been three years old.

He?

She swallowed. *God*. Those things belonged to Tucker.

Was that why none of these physical bios measured up?

She should have been long over him by now. And she'd thought she was. Had thought that having a baby on her own meant she was finally moving forward with her life.

But when he'd stood there on that curb and suddenly grabbed her, she'd come face to face with the flesh and blood man she'd fallen in love with. Passionate and loving, but reserving those feelings for her alone. She hadn't seen that side of him in so long that she'd almost forgotten it existed. And then it had been there. Right in front of her. Making her want to lose herself in his touch.

She hesitated. She'd been disappointed that he hadn't expressed any deeper emotion afterward.

Was it because she was still in love with him?

No. She couldn't be. Not possible when they wanted such different things out of life.

But that was back when the mechanical Tucker had systematically shut her out of his life in the most devastating way imaginable. He'd withheld his touch. His affection. His words of love. They'd inhabited the same physical space but not the same world.

These last three days had been different. It had been like Tucker had woken from a deep slumber.

Could he be changing before her eyes? Or, like her sunglasses, was it all just an illusion?

She didn't know, but she couldn't bank on something that might be confined to her fantasies. Or to a five-day working vacation. She needed permanence. Shared ideals.

Her eyes went back to the last donor's file, turning her phone to the side to see better.

"Must be some interesting reading there."

"Ah!" She let out a scream, the cellphone tumbling out of her hand and landing on the towel she'd tossed down a few minutes earlier. Thank God the pool room was empty this morning.

"Sorry." He bent down to scoop up the phone.

"No, don't—"

Too late. His gaze was on the screen, head cocked to the side. Then twin shutters slammed across his eyes. When they lifted to meet hers there was a blankness she remembered all too well.

The Tucker from the end of their marriage.

"Donor bios? Is this what you were talking about in my office?"

She reached up and grabbed her phone from him. "If you must know, yes."

There was a silence that seemed to stretch on forever.

"Why would you go this route?"

"It's less complicated."

The shutters lifted a little. "Less complicated than what?"

Was he serious? "Than the whole relationship thing. That didn't seem to work out for me all that well."

A muscle pulsed in his jaw. "I'm sorry, Kady. For everything."

No, no, no.

She did not want her future to go hacking around with her past. She needed them to stay in separate realms where she could manage them. When they mixed, things got…complicated. It made those bios look unappealing all over again.

"It doesn't matter. I'm just doing what I think is best for me."

He lowered himself into the chair beside hers. "And going it alone is best?"

"At the moment? Yes."

He nodded at the phone. "Mind if I look?"

"Yes, I mind." She was very aware that she was sitting there clad in nothing but her red bikini. Again. "Did you want something?"

She allowed the crabbiness in her voice to come through. Today had not been the stuff of which dreams were made.

Well, except for that kiss. And even that had turned into a disaster when their medical students had shown up in the middle of it. Just when Tucker had been getting to the good part. And then they'd had to pretend to simply be colleagues for the next two hours while they'd tried to overlap cases without overlapping anything else.

And hell if Kady hadn't wanted to be overlapped. By him. The whole damn time.

She still did, despite her every attempt to banish it from her head.

That was part of the reason she'd decided to come back to the hotel and focus on her future baby. The baby she was going to have.

Not fun. Not fun at all.

She'd been fine with that. Until Tucker had come along with his stupid kisses and super-sexy sofa-loving and ruined it all.

"I actually came by to apologize for coming unglued this morning."

And that was the icing on the cake she'd had in the oven all day. His "coming unglued" was the thing that had given her the most pause about going through with the IVF.

"Nothing to apologize for. It was a kiss. We've certainly done that before."

"Yes, we have." He leaned back and put his hands behind his head, his khaki slacks seeming completely out of place in the steamy humidity of the pool room. "What I'm trying to figure out is why it's happening *now*."

"We're both under a lot of stress right now."

"So you're saying I'm a stress reliever?"

"You're twisting my words out of context." Like him, she had no idea why this was all suddenly happening now, when it hadn't happened three years ago.

He turned his head and nodded toward the phone. "So how many prospects have you got in there?"

Her brain had to hop around a bit to follow his train of thought. This was still none of his business, but maybe by talking about it she could regain her earlier excitement.

"Three." It was insane to be sitting here, discussing this with him.

"I take it all of them are genetically engineered perfection."

"Funny. You're a real funny guy." Okay, now she was mad. Mad because he'd hit on the very nerve she'd been worrying all morning long. How could she even tell what kind of men these were? They might seem like perfect physical specimens, but what were they like? *Who* were they?

She was over-thinking this. People chose sperm donors all the time. And no one ever seemed to regret doing it. At least, not from all the glowing testimonials emblazoned on the walls of the fertility clinic.

"Can I see them?" No sardonic humor in his voice now. He seemed deadly serious.

"Why?"

His dark gaze landed on her. "I'm curious to see who is going to father Grace's half-brother or -sister, that's all."

A shaft of pain went through her. He was right. Any baby she had would be Grace's half-sibling. She would tell them all about her. But she wanted to get one thing straight. "He won't be his or her father. Just a sperm donor."

In reality, the baby wouldn't have a father, just some nameless figure who had masturbated into a plastic cup.

Dammit, why was she making something that should be beautiful into a sleazy backroom thing?

Like her encounter with Tucker in his office?

No, that hadn't been sleazy either. It had been exciting and powerful.

And she was thinking about it far too much to be healthy.

She should be grateful that there were men who were willing to help people like her. They were good, caring men. Men she should be glad had chosen to go this route.

Tucker held his hand out for the phone. Against her better judgment, she handed it to him. "It's kind of hard to read on that format."

"What's your password?"

Her chin tipped up, the numbers rolling off her lips. "Zero-eight-sixteen."

He started to punch the numbers in then stopped.

His Adam's apple jerked up before settling back into place. "August sixteenth. Grace's birthday."

"It seemed appropriate somehow."

"And yet what you're using it for isn't."

A thread of anger uncoiled inside her. "I would have to disagree. She's part of who I am. You admitted yourself that any new child would be Grace's little sister or brother. It's my way of making her a part of the process."

He typed the numbers in and looked at the screen, his thumb and forefinger moving in a way that made her earlier efforts at resizing the wording seem ridiculous.

"Nope. Not this one."

She craned her neck to look at the screen. "Why?" It was one of those Kady had rejected. Maybe Tucker's reasons would be a little more objective.

"He looks like he could be your brother."

Her insides took a dive. Now that he mentioned it, he did look a little bit like the male members of her family.

He scrolled to the next candidate. "A body builder, huh? Is that the type you're drawn to?"

No. It wasn't. But there was no way she was going to tell him who she *was* drawn to. Because it was the man hunched over the small screen, khaki-clad legs on either side of the lounge chair as he kept reading.

He looked gorgeous.

His profile showed a strong nose, a slight bump in the bridge that he said had come from a skateboard accident when he was a teenager.

She couldn't imagine the Tucker of today on a skateboard.

Instead, he frowned. A lot. His serious demeanor had put a dent between his thick brows, wiping away the carefree young man she'd once known. By Grace's death? By their divorce? Or just by life in general?

Could she blame him? She didn't laugh nearly as much as she used to either. Losing a child was an experience that no one should ever have to face.

And Tucker never would again, thanks to his vasectomy.

"What about this third guy?" His voice jerked her attention away, glad he hadn't found her staring at him.

She'd already ruled the fake brother and the body builder guy out. She didn't need to look at this one to know she wasn't going with him either.

How was she going to tell Dr. Torres that she couldn't decide on anyone? Maybe it was like a menu. If there were too many choices, nothing looked good.

Three was hardly too many.

But none of them seemed right.

She was trying to think up an answer when the dent in Tucker's brows became more pronounced. He'd found something he didn't like.

"What is it?"

"Nothing."

That did not look like a nothing kind of expression. "Give me my phone, please. This is ridiculous. You are not going to help me choose a donor."

Surprisingly, he handed it to her. "Thank you."

"So do you accept my apology?"

"Apology for what? Making fun of something that's very serious to me? No."

He swung his legs over the side of the lounge chair and regarded her, elbows on his knees, hands loose between his strong thighs. "I'm not making fun of you, Kady, I know how much this means to you."

A knot formed in her chest. It did. Until now, and she wasn't sure why. "Thank you."

Maybe the mechanical man hadn't returned after all. Actually, he seemed a little different this afternoon, a little softer than when she'd first arrived. Or was that wishful thinking? She'd just been sitting there dreaming about that kiss in front of the hospital and whether or not he'd changed.

Could he have?

His gray eyes moved from her phone to rest on her mouth, as if reading her thoughts. When his attention slid higher, heated shadows now moving through his gaze, she shivered.

He wanted to kiss her. Just like he had in front of the hospital.

"What's happening to us, Tucker? Is it just nostalgia?"

"I didn't behave very well after Grace's death. I think maybe I'm seeing that for the very first time. Some of my choices might not have been very well thought out."

She blinked. Was he talking about having children? "We were both hurting. We just handled it in different ways."

Maybe they'd both been a little impulsive. She'd jumped right to wanting another baby. And he'd leapt in the opposite direction. She might have pushed a little too hard to get her way, but three years after Grace's death her desire to have another child hadn't faded.

"Is that what we're doing now? Handling it? By handling each other?"

She smiled. The first real smile since yesterday. Maybe that's exactly what they'd been doing. And handling hadn't been all that bad. "Maybe it's what we both needed. The question is, now what do we do about it."

Especially since a little voice inside her was whispering to her that they could just keep going on like they were. And after that?

"Hell if I know." His tone was playful, like old times.

Her smile grew. "There are only a few more days left of the conference. Surely we can keep our 'handlings' to ourselves."

"I'm pretty sure about me, but you…?" One side of his mouth went up in the devastating smile he wore so well.

Ha! She wasn't confident about herself either. "Are you saying I might not be able to control myself?"

"I'm saying I know you can't."

She swallowed. He was right. She couldn't. The second he touched her she was toast. Just like she always was.

Not good for a woman contemplating having a child with a complete and utter stranger.

Well, Tucker sure hadn't stepped up and offered his services.

Oh, yes, he had. He might not be able to get her pregnant, but he got the job done. The job of needing and wanting and…

Loving.

Oh, no. No. *No!*

The word games between them had just become deadly serious.

She drew a steadying breath, even as her world tipped from side to side like a rowboat faced with frenzied seas. The reality she'd been toying with earlier washed over the side of her little craft, dumping her into the ocean in a second. She sputtered to the surface and headed back to the overturned vessel as the truth sank in.

She loved him.

That's why none of those applicants seemed right. Why she was looking for some sign of him in each prospect. There wasn't any, because Tucker wasn't in those files.

But it did her no good. She might love him but he didn't love her. Or want children with her.

His very presence was messing with her future happiness.

She needed to tell him in no uncertain terms to stay away from her for the rest of the conference. Otherwise they were in danger of becoming colleagues by day, lovers by night.

"I'm pretty sure I can control myself quite well, thank you very much."

"Really? Let me see that phone again."

"What?"

What had seemed humorous a few minutes ago now left a bad taste in her mouth. He really was okay with letting her go through with using a sperm donor? Not that he had any say in the matter, but after what she'd just realized, it would have been nice to see at least a glimmer of misgivings.

Fine. If he was okay with it, then she would be too.

She handed him the phone. Instead of opening the screen, he set it down on the lounger and then stood to his feet. "What are you doing?"

"Making a point about the boundaries of self-control. It's pretty damned hard to talk about sperm when you're lounging around, wearing practically nothing." He waved his hand over her midsection.

"Nothing? It's called a bikini. This is a pool after all."

"I know. And a bikini and water go together like..." He smiled. A very knowing, cunning smile.

"Don't you dare." She suddenly knew where this was headed.

He scooped her into his arms. "Oh, I dare all right."

"Tucker! Put me down! This is definitely against pool rules."

"It's definitely against our own rules too, but you don't see that stopping me." He started walking toward the edge of the concrete surround.

"Don't."

He paused. "You didn't come out here to swim?"

"Yes, but I changed my mind."

"That's good, because I've changed mine too." He swished her from side to side as he started counting down. "One..."

"No, Tucker, I hate—"

"Two..."

"I am going to kill—"

"Three!"

At the last second she locked her arms around his neck, so that when his hands went to toss her she held tight. If she was going in then so was he, dammit.

They both crashed into the water in a tangle of arms

and legs and shockingly cold water. At least in her boat analogy from earlier, the water had been warm.

She pushed to the surface, checking her bikini top this time before she actually stuck her head out of the water. All secure. Tucker was already at the side of the pool, lifting something out of the water.

His phone! Oh, God. She swam over to him.

"I'm sorry! I had no idea you were carrying that."

He gave her a lopsided grin that carried none of the anger she was expecting. "At least I did you the courtesy of setting yours aside." He shook water droplets from the device, making her cringe.

"Maybe you can put it in a bag of rice or something."

"I don't think rice is going to do any good in this case."

Kady lived on her phone. It had her notes, her contacts, her appointment reminders. Everything. "Did you back it up somewhere?"

As if she did. She never backed up her devices. She would after this, though.

"It's okay. I deserved it. And, yes, it's backed up. And insured."

Was throwing an ex-wife into the pool covered under that particular warranty?

There were lots of things that didn't come with guarantees. Like relationships. And life.

She wished they did, because then, just like the products that lined the shelves, you could avoid those that carried a "buy at your own risk" label. But if she and Tucker had never gotten involved, she wouldn't have those sweet memories of her daughter. The heartache afterward had been almost as horrible as Grace's death, but she would gladly go through it all again if it meant she could hold her baby girl one more time.

But, of course, she couldn't. And there were no do-overs in life. Moaning and groaning about the past did nothing but make you a bitter, angry person.

Like Tucker had been?

If she were honest, she had been pretty bitter and angry herself. About Tucker's attitude, about the fate that had given them both a recessive gene that would destroy not only their daughter's life but also their relationship to each other.

She said the only thing she could think of. "I'll pay to have it repaired."

He tossed the item over to her towel, hitting it on the first try. "I think you already have."

"Ha! Since you were the one who was going to toss me in while you stayed up on the surface high and dry. It seems like you got what was coming to you."

The water had gone from cool to languorously warm as her legs paddled back and forth, her arms supporting her upper body on the side of the pool. Maybe the warmth wasn't so much the water as it was being next to the man she'd been unbelievably intimate with.

With his black polo shirt clinging to his body in all the right places, he was a figure to behold. His khakis were plastered to his legs as well and... "Oh, no. Your shoes!"

"At the bottom of the pool. And they're not insured."

She peered through the water to the bottom and saw two black shapes, one beside the other as if he'd neatly placed them there on purpose. She started laughing, the sound coming up from the depths and carrying across the room. She suddenly felt giddy and care-free—couldn't remember the last time she'd felt this way.

"I'm glad someone finds my monetary outlay funny."

"It just…" She tried to suck down a quick breath before going on, the words broken apart by giggles. "It looks like you planned where each one would land. That's a surgeon for you." Her laughter picked up again, and she had no idea why. It wasn't all that funny. Well, probably not to anyone but her. But Tucker was such a precise man in every way—he liked to be in control of his actions, that tendency carrying over into his surgeries. It's what made him one of the best fetal surgeons in the country.

"It's a good thing I don't invite you in to my surgical suite very often. I don't think my patients would appreciate you chortling your way through their procedures."

"Chortling." She coughed, trying to staunch the weird flow of sounds. "What kind of word is that?"

"It means laughing."

Her nose crinkled as she struggled to regain control over her breathing. Not easy when every time those damn shoes came into her line of vision, her lungs started tightening in preparation for another round.

Not good.

"I know what it means. I've just never heard it used in an actual conversation."

He turned his head to look at her. "There are lots

of words and sounds that aren't used in actual conversations."

Her laughter dried up in a rush.

"Sounds?"

He answered with the lifting of his left brow.

"Boundaries and self-control?"

"Say the word and I'll stay firmly on my side of that line." His finger came up and trailed across her collarbone, belying his words and sending a shudder through her.

He would stop if she asked him to. But right now she was caught under a spell she didn't want to break.

Making a decision, she leaned up to whisper in his ear, "Lines can be stepped across. Can't they?"

"Yes, they can. It's as easy as this." One arm sank beneath the surface of the water and slid across the small of her back, just above her bikini line. "Too far over?"

Unable to trust her voice, she shook her head.

The arm curled around her side, his fingers brushing the indentation of her hip. "How about now?"

"No."

One finger dipped just below the elastic at her waist and stroked just above the juncture of her thighs. When the sensation made her give a low moan, there was no mistaking where this was headed.

He bit her earlobe. "How far across the line am I allowed to go, Kady?"

"A-as far as you want." The words came out thick with need.

Message received.

Tucker's head dipped, his lips seeking and finding hers. All the playful banter of moments earlier disappeared. And something deeper and far more dangerous rose up to take its place. She was ready for it. Had been ready for the last two years.

CHAPTER TEN

THEY CRASHED THROUGH the door of her hotel room, lips still locked, Tucker kicking it shut behind him. It was as if she'd released a latch on some primitive side of him and let loose a beast that was intent on devouring her. And she was more than happy to let him do just that.

The bed was a few feet away, and they fell onto it, Tucker's weight pressing her deep into the mattress. His clothes were wet and chilly against her super-heated skin, but it was okay. She would take whatever she could get of him. His hands went to either side of her face and dark eyes stared into hers. "You're gorgeous. You know that, don't you?"

He made her feel that way.

When she went to draw him back to her, though, he stood, pulling his phone and sodden wallet from his pockets. He then tossed them onto the other side of the king-size bed. Impatient, she sat up, her fingers going to the button on his slacks and making short work of that and the zipper. It took a little bit of ef-fort to see-saw the garment down his lean hips until he could step out of them. "You get your shirt while I get..." She hooked her thumbs into the waistband of his briefs and eased them over the bulge in front. As soon as she did, he sprang free.

God.

She'd almost forgotten how much pleasure this part of his body could bring her. And how much pleasure it could bring him when she touched it. When she...

The hands that had been undoing his shirt stopped the second her lips met his skin. He swore, palm reaching to grip her hair. A half-hearted tug that changed nothing made her smile, although that was hard to do when her mouth was...she opened wide...full.

It was. Full and heavy and incredibly sexy. She loved the intimacy of it. Loved sending him to the brink and watching him try to fight against the rising tide. The thing was, she always won. And he always tried to stop her.

"Kady."

Her gaze went up, brows arching slightly in challenge as her tongue swirled around him. Stroking, tasting, doing everything in her power to make him come unhinged.

Instead, he did the unexpected. He stepped back, breaking the suction. "Not this time."

She licked her lips again. "Not good enough? Then come here so I can do it even better."

"Witch." He came forward, but not to take up where she'd left off. Instead, he reached for her wrists and bore her back to the bed. Arms over her head, he transferred her hands to one of his, then held her in place. "Now it's my turn."

He leaned over her, lips trailing down her neck and collarbone in a way that missed being ticklish by a hair's breadth. Instead it crossed the line into breath-stealing, especially when he cruised the V of her bikini top until he arrived at the other side. And then he found one of her nipples.

Hard, tight, aching.

Breath whooshed from her lungs when he took a long, hard pull on it. Then another.

"I want you so much it hurts."

There was a sound of wonder in his voice that she didn't quite understand, but it didn't matter—she wanted him just as much. Between her legs, inside her, all around her. If she spent her whole life holed up in this room, she wouldn't care.

"Lift your head, honey."

She did as he asked, the fingers of his free hand fumbling with the strings to her bikini. Then he peeled the top down, exposing her breasts. This time, his lips touched bare skin. Her eyes fluttered shut as he teased and nibbled, traveling back and forth. The need inside her expanded faster than she wanted it to, her insides melting. "Tucker, let go of my hands."

His teeth bit down, and she arched up off the bed. "Not yet. Maybe not ever."

She couldn't do anything but moan and thrash as he continued the onslaught, leaving out an important part of her body. And there was nothing to push against to help staunch the growing ache. Her hips pumped into empty air, trying to squeeze her thighs together, anything that would help give her the sensation she was looking for.

He lifted his head and stared down at her. "Spread your legs."

"Not unless you're ready to put something between

them." She didn't recognize the thin, raspy voice that spoke those words.

"Trust me."

She did as he asked, and he moved between them, removing any hope of squeezing herself to orgasm in an instant.

Her groan was met with a smile. "Patience."

A fingertip went to the base of her throat and slowly traveled the midline of her body, between her breasts, down her abdomen, into her bellybutton until he reached the top of her pubic bone. He didn't dive off the edge like she'd hoped. Instead, he zigzagged slowly in place, just above where she wanted it to be.

There was a tenseness in her breasts, her nipples drawn into rigid peaks. They knew what was coming. Only Tucker wasn't giving them the satisfaction that lay just beyond reach. He slid his finger down a smidgen and tracked it back and forth again, a little harder this time.

She moaned, eyes closing. He was so close.

God! *She* was so close.

His voice sounded in her ear, the low, insistent tone adding another tremor to her system. "I'm going to make you come."

There was no doubt of that. She wasn't sure why he was announcing it. She was ready for him to touch her. To *really* touch her.

But a minute went by, then two, while her body strained toward that point of contact. Except there was nothing to push against.

"You're going to come." The voice came again, that finger tracing a circle millimeters away from her pleasure center. "Just with this. Because I need to be inside you. And can't. Until you come. Hard."

She believed him. Already a familiar tingling was gathering speed.

If she thrust her hips hard enough, she might be able to jolt him to the right spot, but she wanted to do this. For him. Wanted his mere presence to send her into the clouds.

"Kady." His tone was now a tense whisper. "I need you to come for me, baby. Please."

It took two seconds, then her body fluttered, a sharp clench of her inner muscles driving her forward. Then another. The spasms and his stroking finger rendered her powerless to retreat to safety, even if she'd wanted to. The next contraction did it.

"Ah-h-h…" She climaxed with a fury that stole her breath. She didn't have time to think about any of that, though, because he was suddenly there inside her, pumping hard and fast, that ravenous beast back to finish off his prey.

"Dammit, yes!" His triumphant oath came just as he let go of her hands and clutched her hips, raising them as he continued to thrust inside of her. "Yes."

He slowed but still pumped, drawing out both their climaxes.

"Yes."

That final word was full of masculine satisfaction. Of satiation.

Drawing a shaky breath, and feeling pretty satisfied herself, she kissed his neck. "You are a very bad man."

He chuckled, making no move to pull away and separate them. "I thought women were drawn to bad boys."

"There is bad and then there is *bad*."

"And which one am I?"

"I haven't decided yet."

He rolled over, drawing her with him. "I can be as bad as you want me to be. Or as good."

Planting her hands on his shoulders, she pushed up so she could look at him. "I can't believe you did that."

"Did what?" He feigned innocence, but his smile said he knew exactly what she was talking about.

"You know."

"It was payback for what you tried to do." His arm hooked around her back, holding her in place. "In fact, I don't think I've been paid in full yet."

He drew his nose up her temple. "Were you picturing any of those donor's faces when I was inside you?"

Was that a hint of jealousy in his voice? "Would that make it more exciting for you?"

"No." The growled word made her laugh.

"We can play who's behind curtain number one."

He kissed the corner of her mouth. "I'm behind all the curtains."

"Are you? Those were supposed to be for the donors. Unless you want to pretend to be one of them. Maybe you're vying for the top spot."

His index finger tickled the lobe of her ear. "And what would you do with me if you chose me?"

"Mmm… I would coax what I needed out of you." She frowned. "Except that's impossible now."

"Let's say things were magically reversed through the wonders of modern technology." His lips pressed against her neck. "Now, how would you coax me?"

Her brain was having a little trouble concentrating, since his mouth had skimmed to her collarbone, his voice low and seductive. "I would use anything I could. My hands. My mouth."

Teeth connected with the sensitive skin at the crook of her neck. When air hissed through her teeth, he licked over the spot, generating a languid warmth that drugged her system. "And after you got it?"

"I'd have to make sure things took, so we might have to make multiple attempts."

"Multiple attempts. Oh, yes, I think we would. And once it took? Would you throw me away?"

"Never."

His fingers found one of her nipples, wrenching a moan out of her. "So now you have me. And you've coaxed and coaxed and coaxed. What comes next?"

Her breath was coming in shorter spurts. "W-we'd have to get busy, choosing names."

"Bueller." He squeezed the tight peak of her breast, making her writhe against him.

"No."

"No, Kady? Are you sure?" The pad of his thumb brushed over her and her eyes fluttered closed.

"No to Bueller. Not to that."

"How about Gregorian?" The pressure of his thumb increased slightly.

"Isn't Gregorian…a type…of chant?" She was doing some chanting of her own and it had nothing to do with baby names. "Why are we only having boys?"

A sense of euphoria was making it increasingly hard for her to think. This was a conversation he never would have participated in three years ago. And now he was smiling. Kissing her. Thinking up outrageous names, even as he was driving her wild with need. Was this their new normal? She hoped so.

"We're only having boys because…" His hands moved to her hips, shifting her just a little to the left. Something magically began stirring down below. "Right on cue. Saved by the hoisting of the mainsail. And it didn't need any coaxing after all."

She gave an over-dramatic sigh that sounded more like a whimpered plea. "You're taking all the fun out of it."

Actually, he wasn't. He was putting all the fun back into her life. Fun that she'd almost thought obliterated forever.

"Want to bet?" He positioned her, thrusting upward in a rush.

She gasped as he filled her completely. "Didn't you just…?" Her voice squeaked to a stop when his palms glided over her backside and squeezed. "You can't mean to…"

"I can." He smiled up at her. "And I do. Maybe it's time I did a little coaxing of my own."

Coaxing. It had worked. A little too well.

Tucker needed to wake her up, even though it was the last thing he wanted to do. But they had missed their conference session, spending the afternoon making love again and again instead. He was exhausted. In a good and familiar way. A way that once upon a time he'd thought he'd never feel again.

Those days were over.

At least, he hoped they were.

Were they falling in love all over again? If so, what did he do about it? He could stop it in its tracks with well-placed flippancy once those gorgeous green eyes opened.

But he didn't want to do that. He didn't want to hurt her.

So what *did* he want to do?

What he wanted to do and what he *should* do might be two different things. He had to tread carefully. Maybe he could start by reexamining some of his choices. And sharing those with her. He'd tried to do a little of that during the game they'd played this afternoon, hopefully letting her know that he really did want to be behind the curtain.

Kady squirmed in her sleep, a soft sigh and a puckering of her lips making him wonder if she was dreaming about what they'd done together. His gaze trailed over the naked line of her back and the spot just above her ass where the edge of the sheet rested.

The same finger that he'd used last night went behind her ear, brushing back and forth over the tender skin. As much as he wanted to stay here with her all night, his stomach was beginning to protest that, at seven thirty, it was past his dinnertime.

He leaned down and replaced his finger with his lips, dropping tiny kisses behind her ear, her scent drifting up in intoxicating little eddies. She murmured something unintelligible and tilted her head closer, as if seeking out his touch. His body stirred all over again.

God, he loved this woman.

The kisses stopped.

Loved.

Loved.

He did. Had never stopped. He'd just buried those emotions beneath a load of fear when all the talk of babies had started.

But she still wanted children. Was looking to find a sperm donor to get her there.

Maybe she would rethink that. Especially after their afternoon play date.

Was that what he wanted? To make her change her life plans so they could be together?

Maybe. Would she be willing to? Or maybe he was the one who needed to be willing to change. He'd meant what he'd said about being behind all of those curtains.

He wanted her to choose him. Even if it was on her terms? Playing around with baby names hadn't been as gut-wrenching as it had been at one time. In fact, it had been—

"Tucker." She groaned his name, and his body hardened further. He loved hearing her say his name in that cute, almost-accented tone. Especially when it came in on one of those breathy little sighs that said she liked whatever he was doing.

He kissed her again. "Time to wake up. We have somewhere to be."

"Somewhere to be?" Her eyes blinked open and she rolled onto her back, her breasts gloriously exposed to his gaze.

Right now the only place he wanted to be was in this bed with her.

"We are going out to dinner."

"Mmm…" Her eyes met his. The spot between her brows puckered as she processed that thought. Then she sat up, her frown growing deeper. "What time is it?"

"Seven thirty."

"Oh, no! We missed the conference. And it's the last night. Why didn't you wake me up?"

He smiled. "I believe I was trying to do just that. I'm insulted that my kisses didn't have more of an effect."

She muttered something under her breath.

"What was that?"

"Nothing."

That adorable just-woken grumpiness. He even missed that.

His lips pressed against her temple. "Maybe my kisses were having an effect after all. Was that the problem?"

"No."

He nipped the edge of her jaw, moving just close enough to her mouth to make her wonder. "Are you sure?"

"Do we really have to eat?" She turned slightly until they were lined up lip to lip. "Because if the answer is no, you could just lie back and let me demonstrate some truly effective kissing techniques. Or there's always pole dancing with a very special pole."

The groan this time was all his. "Don't go there, Kady."

She laughed. "You are so transparent."

A slight cloud came over him. Hell, she probably could see right through him. Maybe even knew that he loved her. If so, why did she find that amusing? Because nothing about what he'd just realized was funny.

At least, not to him.

A thread of warning coiled around his heart. He should just tell her how he felt and see if she felt the same way.

Their time together was almost over. If he was going to confess, it needed to be now—tonight—or she would disappear back to Atlanta and he would miss his chance.

You already missed your chance.

The whispered words went through his head and the string tightened further.

He ignored it, glancing at the clock next to the bed. "I want to go someplace fancy. But for the place I'm thinking of, we need to be there by eight thirty. Did you bring a dress?"

The big confessions could wait until they'd eaten. Or during dinner. Maybe once he had some food in his stomach the memories of last night wouldn't clog his thoughts. He needed to be clearheaded about what was best for the both of them. Even if he hadn't yet figured that out.

Still, it couldn't hurt to drop little hints, could it? Threading his fingers through her hair, he turned her head again and kissed her, the cling of her lips filling him with wonder. Okay, they were both awake. Their sex drive had been satisfied and she was still willing to kiss him. Scratch that. Satisfied for the moment. Because he was back to wanting her every moment of the day.

This time it was Kady who whispered. "Fifty-nine minutes until the witching hour. And, yes, I brought a dress. A slinky red one, as a matter of fact."

He didn't want to know what had possessed her to pack something sexy. Had she been planning to go to a club and meet men? When a frisson of what he knew to be jealousy crawled through his gut, he pushed it away with a shake of his head. What did it matter, as long as she used that dress on him?

"Ugh." He swung out of the bed with a muttered curse. "I guess it really is time to get moving. Do you want the shower first?"

"No, you go ahead. I need to dig some clothes out of my suitcase."

"I don't like you in clothes."

She laughed again. "Wasn't it you who said the hospital might frown if I showed up for rounds in a bikini? Or, worse, naked? I think they would be equally upset if we were pulled over for a traffic stop, and they saw I was sitting there without a stitch of clothing on."

"It might get us out of a ticket." But that thin thread of jealousy was rearing its ugly head again. On second thoughts, he wanted her in clothes whenever they were outside the bedroom.

"How about if you were out of a job afterward, if the hospital caught wind of it? I know how much you like to eat."

"I *love* to eat." He said it with a wicked lift of his brows that had her out of bed in a flash.

"Later. Right now, you need to go get your shower, so we can both eat." Before he had a chance to think of a rejoinder, she added, "At that restaurant you mentioned."

He scooped his clothes off the floor. Damn, he didn't have any clean clothes here in her hotel room. It didn't matter. They'd have to swing by his apartment anyway, so he could put a suit on. Danali's was fancy enough to have a strict dress code. He went there about once a week, mostly for business meetings, but something made him want to show it off to Kady. Or maybe it was just that he wanted to show her off.

He got in the shower and lathered up quickly. Those tight cords he'd housed in his chest for the last three years were cut in two by a burst of true happiness. She hadn't acted weird or stilted or awkward or any of those things that could have occurred once she'd woken up. They had played and laughed and made love just like they used to.

Could they make this work? For real this time?

He was dried and dressed in ten minutes, brushing his teeth with the complimentary toothbrush in a plastic wrapper he found propped in a cup. Another toothbrush was nearby, this one not covered by plastic. He dropped his in next to hers.

Looked good. Right.

As did the thought of sleeping in her bed every night.

Something pinged in the back of his head. Nope, not going to think about it. Not right now. Whatever happened when her time in New York ended, he could at least enjoy being with her right now.

He would worry about tomorrow...

Tomorrow.

Tucker looked gorgeous in his black suit. With his dark hair slicked back from his broad forehead and freshly shaven, he had taken all of ten minutes to get ready. Even so, they had barely made the eight-thirty cutoff. But it probably wouldn't have mattered. The waitstaff knew him and seated them immediately.

How often did he come here anyway? And who did

he come with? Probably not a colleague slash lover. At least, not if he was smart.

She'd learned the hard way that interhospital relationships were not a good idea. Another doctor had asked her out on a date soon after her and Tucker's divorce. She'd turned him down in the nicest way possible, but the man had kept coming back for more over the next several weeks. She'd finally had to tell him point blank that she wasn't interested. And then it had started. The harassing phone calls. Going to her patients and making little digs about her with thinly veiled hints that she was incompetent.

It had taken a patient complaint to make him lose privileges at the hospital. But it was something she hadn't forgotten. Now she simply remained as aloof as possible with male colleagues. She was sure there was whispering about that behind her back as well, but at least it kept them away. It was difficult and went against her character. In hardening her heart, she had become almost like... Tucker.

That made her smile. Because Tucker was not acting very Tucker-like right now. He was anything but aloof, his glances holding a smoldering promise that said there might be more of this afternoon headed her way tonight. And that was fine with her.

She fluffed her napkin on her lap and accepted the menu the waiter handed her. "Thank you."

She tried to study the choices, but the words blurred until they were undecipherable.

How long could they keep this up?

She swallowed. Not very long. She was scheduled to fly out of New York tomorrow afternoon.

She didn't want to go. A complete turnaround from that first day, when she hadn't wanted to stay.

"Do you see anything that interests you?"

She glanced up. Yes, she did. And it was sitting across the table from her. But there was no way she was going to say that. "Do you have any suggestions? It seems you come here quite often."

"I do. But only for business reasons. Meetings with hospital bigwigs or sponsors." He reached over and took her hand. "I'm glad I'm not the only one."

"I'm sorry?"

"I was worried about your reasons for packing that dress."

She glanced down. The red silk creation, with its spaghetti straps and curve-hugging fabric had been a last-minute addition to her luggage. She'd somehow thought she might have time to catch a show on Broadway. Little had she known that every spare second would end up being spent in the company of this man. But, oh, was she glad it had wound up that way.

"I'd hoped to catch one of the musicals New York is famous for."

"Alone?"

She blinked. "Of course. Who would I have gone with?"

"No one." He squeezed her hand. "I wish I'd known. I'd have taken you."

"You would?"

The thought of actually sitting beside Tucker at a Broadway musical made her heart flutter. With nerves? With anticipation? She wasn't sure what she felt right now. Forcing a cheery note into her voice, she said, "Next visit?"

He paused and studied her. "Why does this visit have to end?"

"I'm scheduled to fly out after our meeting with the students, for one thing."

She waited for him to respond, only to be disappointed when the waiter appeared to ask if they were ready to order. Kady gave Tucker a nod, hoping he would order for her. He knew what she liked.

Yes, he did. In more ways than one.

Maybe it was time for them to have a heart-to-heart talk and see what happened.

And if he loved her? Did she dare hope? He'd certainly talked last night like he wanted a future with her. That wasn't the only surprising thing. The talk about reversing his vasectomy had sent shockwaves through her system. She'd thought he was joking. Until he'd started naming any children he might father. Yes, the names had been outrageous. But at one time this topic of conversation would have been off limits. In fact, they wouldn't have made it past the mention of babies.

This was a whole new playing field, it would seem. But what did it mean?

He'd hinted that some of his decisions after Grace's death might have been impulsive. Did that include his vasectomy? Was that why he'd mentioned having it reversed?

They'd talked more about Grace this week than almost ever before, but past experience still had her tiptoeing around the subject. Maybe it was time to test the waters again.

As soon as the waiter poured their wine, she took a careful sip.

"I think we should talk about things."

He nodded. "I have a few things I'd like to talk about as well."

That surprised her. But at least he seemed willing to open up and have an actual conversation. At least she hoped they both had the same topic on their minds.

"Why don't you go first?"

There was a pause while Tucker repositioned his cutlery. Stalling. She could certainly understand that. None of this was easy—for either of them. Finally he glanced up at her.

"I think I'd like you to reconsider going through with the in vitro procedure. And to reconsider going back to Atlanta."

"You want me to stay here? With you?"

"Yes."

She swallowed hard. It couldn't be this easy. Could it?

Oh, God, what if it was? What if it really, truly was?

Pulling up to the curb in that taxi and exiting in their evening dress had seemed like some kind of fairy tale. The twinkle lights at the front of the restaurant, the formal waitstaff, the quiet intimate atmosphere all contributed to that feeling. If Tucker had planned for this to be a new start, he couldn't have chosen a better venue.

This was the moment of truth. To bare her soul and see what happened. She paused to take another sip of her drink. A bigger one this time, needing a shot of courage. "So you were serious about all of that stuff you said last night?"

"I was never more serious in my life."

She set her glass down, the breath catching in her

lungs. "You're actually willing to have the procedure reversed?"

He looked at her, head cocking to the left, his warm and sexy expression gradually fading until careful neutrality was all that remained. "Reversed?"

"Your vasectomy."

Neutral went to something a little darker. Was that fear around the edges of his pupils? Or just dismay? "I never said I was going to have it reversed."

"You did. I heard you."

"You mean when we were in bed?" He sat back in his chair. "It was a hypothetical situation. We were pretending. About a lot of things. Remember?"

Pretending? Yes, they had been. But she'd thought there had been at least a modicum of truth buried beneath all that pretense. Like him being the one she chose.

Hell, they'd made love as if nothing else had mattered. And he'd joked about falling back into bed tonight. Like they were on the cusp of a new beginning.

As if nothing had happened in their past.

Was that it?

He was willing to pretend that none of those bitter times had ever happened.

And what about Grace? Did he want to pretend she had never happened either?

That was not an option. He might like games of make-believe, but there were some things she wasn't willing to wave a magic wand at.

And what about future children? Had she misunderstood those veiled hints. Maybe he hadn't been talking about that at all.

"What else were you pretending about, Tucker?"

She lifted her chin. "Or did this week not mean anything besides sex?"

"You know that's not true. I asked you to stay in New York not five minutes ago." A grain of irritation had appeared in his voice.

"You also asked me to reconsider having the IVF treatment. Why, if you're not going to have the vasectomy reversed?"

There was a longer pause this time. So long that she could hear her heartbeat in her ears, hear the exact moment it began picking up speed.

"I was seeing where things stood."

The pounding in her chest became a low roar. "Would it be a problem if I said I still wanted to go through with it?" Maybe he was just worried about the risks involved in getting things reversed. Even as she thought it, the rational side of her rejected that possibility.

She didn't want to be rational. Not about this. She wanted the fairy tale, dammit! She wasn't quite willing to give up on it just yet. He wanted her to stay. Surely they could work something out?

Then he touched her cheek. "Can you live without it, Kady?"

All her hopes washed out in a split second, leaving behind an ugly, slippery stain.

"Are you asking me to?"

"I thought I could consider the possibility—"

"Consider?"

As in merely tolerating the idea? The last time they'd gone down this road, she'd begged and pleaded for him to change his mind. It had gotten her nowhere. And now he'd moved only as far as considering it?

After all those words to the contrary earlier today?

Like he'd said, they'd only been words. Just a whole lot of pretend. Had he thought it would make her even hotter for him?

It had. Oh, Lord, it had.

Her eyes watered, and her hands clenched the napkin in her lap. She willed the tears not to spill over.

Never again. Not with this man. She would not fight this battle a second time.

She might have acquiesced if there'd been any kind of actual give and take on the subject. But there hadn't been.

Raw anger clutched her innards, making it hard to speak. But she had to.

"I'm sorry, Tucker, that's not good enough." Her clenched hands moved to the top of the table. "I'll lay this out as plainly as I can, so there are no more misunderstandings. I am going through with the IVF treatments. With your blessing or without it."

If he was stunned, he didn't show it. He simply nodded. "I thought that might be the case. I'm happy for you, of course."

Said as if she were an acquaintance who had shared a bit of good news with him. No "we" anywhere in there.

God, how could she have been so stupid? This afternoon she'd been so sure he was reexamining their relationship the same way she was, hoping that maybe somewhere in their individual plans there was room for something more. Something lasting.

If she was going to kill the dream, she was going to kill it completely.

"So that means you're not interested in children. Not ever."

His gaze held steady. Too steady. Robot Tucker had taken up residence again.

"I think I made that pretty clear three years ago."

He had. And she was a fool to think that might have changed over the course of a week.

With the tears still lingering in the background, she tried to think of some way to avoid going down opposite sides of the highway. She looked for some kind of intersection. A fork in the road. Anything that might mean their worlds might be able to meet in some way, shape or form. All she saw were two parallel lanes that stretched as far as the eye could see.

There was no bridge. No crossroad. No body of water connecting the two, and there was a space in between that was impossible to leap across.

How was she going to survive meeting with those students in the morning when all she wanted to do was get on a plane and run home?

"You did. You made it crystal-clear."

And she was done. So very done. In more ways than one. With this trip. With this dinner. With this man.

She stood to her feet, dropping her napkin onto the table in front of her.

"I think this is where we part ways once again. I'm going back to Atlanta. Just like I planned." Drawing in a deep breath, she was aware that people were beginning to glance her way, but she didn't care. "And since you enjoy pretending so much, I'll let you in on a little secret. Once I get home, I'm going to pretend that none of this ever happened. I bet I'll even fool myself in the process. After all, I had the best teacher around."

With that, she turned and walked away, throwing the waiter a shaky smile as she passed him. When he made to say something, she held up her hand to stop him. "Unfortunately, I think Dr. Stephenson has decided to change his reservation at the last minute. He's now officially a party of one."

CHAPTER ELEVEN

SHE WAS GONE. And Tucker was sitting in his car alone.

He couldn't believe she'd left without so much as a goodbye—although after the way she stormed out of the restaurant last night, he should have had a pretty good inkling of what was coming.

He hadn't gone after her, partly because he'd been stunned that she'd thought he'd been serious yesterday about the vasectomy thing.

He hadn't been, had he?

It had started out as a hypothetical situation, but by the end even he'd had a hard time differentiating between fantasy and reality. So he couldn't blame her for being confused.

But to just walk away?

He'd thought she would at least show up for their rounds with the medical students. A little voice had warned him that probably wasn't going to happen.

Even so, he and the students had waited for her for a good fifteen minutes before a niggle in the back of his mind told him to call the hotel. When they'd patched him through to her room the number had rung and rung and rung. And he didn't have her damn cell-phone number anymore, because the pool water had wiped everything in his cellphone clean. His phone wouldn't even start up. And to go to the department head meant an awkward explanation as to why he wanted to call her.

By that evening she'd checked out of the hotel and was gone. Because of him.

He sat in his car, toying with his new replacement phone. All his contact information had been saved to the cloud—who knew?—so he had her number again. Unless she'd changed it.

So why hadn't he tried to call?

Because deep in his heart he knew it wouldn't change anything. It was about her wish to have children. The second he'd realized she was serious, he'd panicked, just like he had in the past. All his vows not to act rashly had been wiped away in the course of a single sentence.

Can you live without it?

He knew Kady well enough to know that it would take a force of nature to change her course.

Maybe the correct question should have been, could he live *with* it?

After they'd made love, the answer would have been…maybe. Until she'd mentioned the reversal, then when he shot that down, she'd said she was going through with the IVF.

Kady wasn't looking to repeat their experience with Grace. He knew her well enough to know she'd be careful beyond belief either with screening the embryo before implantation, or if she went the IVF route, screening the donor with equal care. So her child wouldn't have any genetic anomalies if she could help it.

So what was the real problem? Was it children in general? Or was it that he had never come to terms with Grace's death?

Staring at the church across the way, he drew in a deep breath, because he already knew the answer. What he decided in the next few minutes would set the course for the rest of his life.

Could he live with it?

Maybe the time had come to find out once and for all.

He'd looked up support groups, surprised to find one that met less than ten miles from the hospital.

Whether he could go in or not remained to be seen.

To stay or leave.

Kady had left.

But in his case, leaving would be the coward's way out. In her case, it had been because she'd seen no hope for the future.

He could go back to life as it had been—keep sending anonymous flowers to Grace's grave without actually dealing with the deep pain caused by her loss.

The three years since her death had been miserable.

Until Kady had walked back into his life with her eternal optimism and a smile that had turned him inside out. She'd somehow been able to come to grips with what had happened to Grace. At least he thought she had. So why couldn't he?

Someone parked beside him and a young couple got out of the car. The woman clutched a book that reminded him of…a photo album. He looked down at his own empty hands.

He didn't have one. The only thing he had was a faded mental image of what his child had once looked like. When he'd come to New York, he'd left everything behind, intending to start a new life.

He hadn't. Not really. He'd just coasted along, bouncing from patient to patient, until it had all become a big blur.

The couple walked up the steps to the church. It was then that he realized the woman was pregnant, the wind plastering her shirt to her rounded belly and giving her away. He frowned. Were they going to the same meeting as he was? He glanced at his watch. It was supposed to start in five minutes.

Stay? Or leave?

He counted down the minutes. He reached the minute and a half mark before he released the latch on the door and stepped onto the pavement. Then, with a tightness in his chest and a queasy sensation in his gut, he walked up the steps and opened the door.

There were eight people seated in a circle. Three couples and two people by themselves. At a long table a woman was arranging pamphlets. In a dark skirt and a white blouse, she had an official look to her. That must be the leader of the support group. She turned and caught sight of him and walked over with an extended hand.

"Hello. I don't think we've met. I'm Nadya Rosenberg. Are you here for the Tay-Sachs meeting?"

She said the word matter-of-factly, no hesitation, as if it was something she said every day. Maybe she did.

"Tucker Stevenson. And, yes, I'm here for the meeting."

"Feel free to pick a seat. We'll get started in just a minute."

He picked a chair as far from the couple with the

photo album as he could, not that there were a hundred places to choose from.

Nadya opened with some announcements about upcoming events and learning opportunities.

Opportunities? He'd assumed that everyone in this group had lost a child to the disease.

"So last week we talked a little bit about genetic counseling. Did any of you have a chance to do that or find out more? Or, if you've been, can you tell us your experience?"

A couple of people said they were looking into it. He glanced at the couple who were expecting a baby, wondering what their story was. Maybe they'd lost a nephew or niece and not a child.

Once that topic of conversation petered out, Nadya redirected the group to something else. Just when he'd decided that this wasn't going to benefit him at all, she turned to the couple with the album.

"Heidi, why don't you share what you told me after the session last week?"

Fingers gripping the book in her lap, her husband put an arm around her shoulders and gave her an encouraging nod.

"Well. Most of you know that we're going to have a baby, and if not…well, it's pretty obvious."

A few chuckles met her words.

She smiled. "I wanted to share that losing a child to Tay-Sachs doesn't mean you can never have another baby. I mean, I'm not trying to tell anyone how to…" Her voice faded away.

"This is your story, Heidi. Yours. There are no judgments here."

She smoothed a hand across the book. "We lost

Logan—our first child—ten years ago. We were devastated obviously. We still miss him. That will never change."

Several people nodded.

"We don't regret having him. He brought us so much happiness in the four years he was with us." She opened to the first page of the album. "I recorded everything I could, especially after the diagnosis. I'm here to say it's okay to be sad. To be angry. To put life on hold for a while."

She took a breath. "But you can't do it forever. I did, for ten long years. Until I realized that Logan would be horrified at the way I set my whole life orbiting around him, long after he was gone. We went through counseling—and it was the best and hardest thing I've ever done in my life.

"This new baby is going to be a girl. Could she have Tay-Sachs? No. Because we had the embryo tested before implantation. But she could be born with something equally devastating. Or get cancer. Or die in a car accident." Her glance touched on him and then skipped away.

"Life has to be lived. With all its happiness. And all its terrifying uncertainty."

She might have been speaking directly to Tucker, even though he sensed she wasn't trying to convince anyone of anything.

The woman's chin quivered for a second and her husband whispered something in her ear. She nodded. "If anyone wants to see pictures of Logan, feel free. Just know that you can't stop living. Educate yourself, yes. But live. For our children's sakes. Don't make them the punctuation mark that ends your story. Life goes on. Yes, stop. Take time. As much time as you need. But don't let it stop you from celebrating life. Theirs. And yours."

One of the people next to her asked to see the album and it started to make its way around the circle. Tucker watched as people smiled at whatever was in that book. He hoped he could get out of there before it reached him.

Nadya glanced his way. "I know you're new, and if you don't want to say anything it's okay. But if you do, we're here to listen and help each other. Tay-Sachs has touched all our lives in some way. Do you want to tell us how it touched yours?"

He sat there for a long moment. That moment turned into two. As he looked around at the faces in the room, he saw...understanding. Maybe all that pretending with Kady that day had been his subconscious, telling him it was okay to let the past go. To look to a new future...with a woman he loved. And that having children didn't mean he loved Grace any less.

Suddenly he wanted it all. To laugh with Kady as they chose outrageous baby names. And to be willing to deal with the nitty-gritty—and sometimes painful—business of living, in between all that laughter.

Then the book landed on his lap. A photo of a towheaded little boy graced the cover of it. Probably a year old and still able to smile, he was dressed in a blue and white sailor suit. Tucker stared at the picture, unable to look away. A celebration of life, she'd said. Of her child's life.

Maybe he should start celebrating Grace's life. And beyond that?

His fingers closed around the album, gripping it so tightly he half expected it to break in two.

And after that, maybe he should allow himself to be open to the possibility that he might be able to experience the joy he'd once felt with Grace…with another child.

Kady should be here. He should have called her and asked her to come. They could have gone through this together.

And maybe they still could.

If he hadn't completely destroyed any possibility of that.

Taking a deep breath, he passed the photo album on to the next person and leaned forward. "I had a daughter. Her name was Grace. She had blond hair. Blue eyes. And the most beautiful smile you've ever seen."

Kady felt no different than she had a week ago in her doctor's office. Except now she had two tiny embryos inside her. And a lingering numbness that had nothing to do with the procedure and everything to do with her ex-husband. Every day, she'd wondered the same thing: Had she done the right thing in leaving like she had?

But how could she have stayed?

Tucker had made it more than clear that he hadn't changed his mind. Hadn't the actual vasectomy warned her of that?

Evidently not, because she'd allowed her hopes to creep up. Then she'd taken his words about having it reversed as fact, only to have Tucker roll down his steel doors, locking her out. Locking everyone out.

Just like before.

She wasn't willing to go through that kind of pain ever again. Not even for the man she loved. The sex had been great. The emotional cleanup afterward... not so much.

She dropped into her office chair. Her twelve-hour shift was just ending, and all she wanted to do was go home and sleep. Maybe that was the hormones talking. Or maybe it was just normal physical and emotional exhaustion. The top of her desk looked pretty damn attractive right now. She could just put her head down and take a few hours to recharge before heading home.

Except it brought back memories of a few hours spent in another office in another city. Where she'd made love to a man she'd once considered her soul mate.

Her cellphone chirped a text at her, and she groaned aloud. Please, don't let there be another emergency. So far she'd dealt with one crisis after another. And that didn't include the ones in her personal life.

She glanced at the screen. Needed at nursery. Can you come?

No name was attached to the message, just a phone number. That was weird. Maybe it was the parent of one of her neonates. She often gave parents her cellphone number in case one of them had questions. It relieved their minds to know she was within reach.

Sighing, she stood and stretched her back and then smiled. If she thought her back ached now, just wait a few more months when those babies started growing. "Please stay put, little ziggies." The embryos had grown past the zygote stage, but the pet name had stuck. She went down a floor and exited the elevator, turning left only to stop dead in her tracks.

She swallowed. Okay. Exactly how tired was she?

Pretty damn tired, unless the hormones were causing her to hallucinate.

Tucker stood in front of her, holding what looked like a pink balloon in the shape of a heart.

Neither of them moved. She tilted her head to the side, hoping he would blink into nothingness before she did something stupid. Like rush into his arms. Or start blubbering. Hormones. It had to be.

He didn't disappear. But he wasn't smiling either. Why was he here?

"Did I leave something in New York?"

If that wasn't the dumbest line ever. If she'd left something, the hotel or hospital would have just mailed it. They wouldn't have sent Tucker. And she was *not* going to ask about the balloon. Maybe he was visiting someone in the nursery.

Oh, God, had he fathered a child with someone else?

You really need to get a grip, Kady. He made it pretty clear he was never getting that procedure reversed.

"It's not what you left. It's what you *didn't* leave."

She didn't what? It took her a second to realize he was answering her question. "I don't understand."

"You forgot to leave me a little wiggle room—or a chance to do the right thing."

He hadn't taken a step toward her, and she realized there was more than one person staring at them. Just like at that restaurant. She swallowed.

"Let's go to my office."

"I'd rather do this here." He glanced to the side. "But we can go over by the windows if you'd like."

"Okay." He led the way across the room, that ridiculous balloon bouncing with every step he took. She stopped next to him, gazing out over the park for a minute, then she turned back to him. If he was here to talk her out of it, he needed to know he was too late.

"Before you say anything, I want to let you know that it's already done."

"What is?"

She clasped her hands in front of her, not because she was embarrassed but because she had to steel herself not to touch him. "I had two embryos implanted last week."

"Okay."

She tried to read something into his tone. Panic. Anger. Resignation. But there was nothing. Nothing that she could sense, anyway.

"Okay? Just okay? Is that all you have to say?"

"No. I have a whole lot to say."

She shrugged. "I don't know what you could possibly say that would make a difference at this point."

"Maybe not, but I need to at least tell you this. I didn't mean what I said at dinner. I was stupid. And tired." He took a step closer. "And terrified."

"You shut me down the second I tried to talk to you about it. Just like you did when we lost Grace. I'm sorry I misunderstood about the vasectomy thing, but can you at least see how I could have gotten that idea?"

"I do."

Okay, it was a start.

"I'm not sure they're both going to take, but I want these babies, Tucker. Not to replace Grace. They could never do that. But I can't live my life in the shadow of her memory. And you shouldn't either."

"I know that now. And I think I finally understand."

She doubted it, but if that's what he wanted to think, good for him. "You came all this way to tell me that?"

"No. I came to give you this." He placed the string of the balloon in one of her hands and closed her fingers around it.

Had he somehow heard about her pregnancy before he'd come? He only had one balloon so probably not. "What is this for?"

"You said this was something you were going to do. With my blessing or without it. I know you don't need it, but I wanted you to know that you have it." He paused again. "I went to a support group for the families of Tay-Sachs patients."

Shock rippled across her belly. "You did?"

He nodded. "I told them about Grace. About us. About all of it."

"You...you..."

She had a sudden need to sit down, so she dropped into the nearest chair, fighting the urge to put her head between her knees.

You are not going to faint.

He'd actually told someone about their daughter? That was...it was...

Unbelievable.

She gripped the string of the balloon, afraid to let go. He'd said it was his blessing. For children?

"What made you want to go?"

"It was time. It was past time." His fingers wrapped around hers. "I lost you once. I didn't want to lose you again. I hope I haven't."

He wasn't making any sense. "You don't want children."

"I didn't. The thought scared the hell out of me. So much so that when you talked about it all those years ago, I froze. I couldn't touch you because I was afraid you would get pregnant. It got to the point that I wouldn't have physically been able to make love to you, even if I'd wanted to."

"You didn't want to. That much was obvious." The pain of those days came rushing back.

"I did. But my body wasn't going to cooperate. I simply couldn't perform. The long and the short of it was that I didn't deal with Grace's death the way I should have. I pushed it away and tried to forget it ever happened. And then I pushed you away as well."

"Why the vasectomy?"

"I'd told myself that if I could take away the fear of an accidental pregnancy I could get back to normal. But you were so against my having the procedure that we both said things we shouldn't have. Things got tangled into a knot that neither of us could untie."

"I thought you no longer wanted me. It almost killed me."

"I never stopped wanting you. Ever. And I'm sorry that I didn't talk to you about it. I was embarrassed and angry. At the world. At the doctors." He raised their joined hands and kissed her fingers. "At myself. So am I too late?"

"I think so, as I'm pregnant." Those words should tell him all he needed to know. She wouldn't go back and undo it, even if she could.

He smiled. "What if I said I'm finally okay with that?"

"Are you?" Something had gotten lost in translation here. The last time she'd seen him, nothing had changed. He hadn't wanted children. Had only *pretended* to want them. Was he still pretending?

"I once asked you if you could live without it, Kady. What I should have been asking was if I could live with it. I came to the conclusion at the support group that I can. I think maybe my heart knew it, but my thick skull just couldn't process it."

"What?" Okay, maybe her head really was lying on her desk and she was deep in some kind of dream world.

"I'm still scared as hell, Kady. But I'm here to tell you I'm on board on hundred percent. I want the baby—babies—you're carrying."

"Y-you're okay with becoming a father again?"

"The support group was the first step in healing, I think. But yes." His smile grew. "You really have two of them in there? I guess I should have brought more balloons."

She felt she had to warn him. "There are no guarantees that they'll take."

"I know. I'm willing to risk it. If you are pregnant or not, I still want you in my life. And if both of these babies make it, then I want them in my life too."

A sliver of sunlight came through one of the windows and hit the floor in front of her, and she allowed herself to hope. "Are you sure?"

"Yes. I am."

She closed her eyes, and thanked whatever gods were looking down at them. When she opened them again, Tucker was still there. Strong and steady. The Tucker she'd fallen in love with.

"Where do you want me?"

His head shifted sideways to look at her. "Excuse me?"

She laughed. "I mean, where do we live? Here in Atlanta? Or do you want to go back to New York? Maybe my grandparents could be talked into relocating, since they're ready to downsize."

"So you're willing to give me a second chance?"

She let go of the balloon and watched as it drifted toward the high ceiling above. "I've been willing for a very long time."

"You're going to be sorry you did that." He nodded toward the balloon. "Because now we're going to have to go after it."

"I'm sure it'll come down eventually."

"I'm sure it will, but since your wedding rings are in there we might want to make sure we're here when it does."

"My wedding rings?"

He nodded. "Although if you don't want any reminders of the past, I'll understand. We can always buy a new set."

"I loved those rings."

"And I love you, Kady. We'll get the balloon back. Once I do this." He lowered his head and captured her lips in a kiss that was sweet, gentle and filled with a longing she understood far too well.

She would have told him she loved him too, but her mouth was busy at the moment. And she figured there would be plenty of time for that. And for decisions about where to live. And to catch that runaway balloon.

They had their whole lives ahead of them.

And if they were very, very lucky, they would have the lives of two special babies to celebrate somewhere along the way.

EPILOGUE

THE MOMENT HE held his newborn daughter, he knew it was going to be okay.

And she *was* his daughter, no matter what any paternity test might say. The rush of love he'd been so afraid he wouldn't be able to feel came hurtling toward him, stopping right at his feet. Just like his love for her mother.

"She's gorgeous." He pressed her tiny form to the skin of his chest, the contact branding him for life. They hadn't done this with Grace, and he was glad Kady had insisted on him unbuttoning his shirt before he held her. He was also glad she'd so steadfastly said she wanted a baby. With or without him.

He'd chosen with.

It was the right choice. He knew it.

In the end Kady had chosen both sperm and eggs from donors, just so there would be no chances.

He smiled. And both embryos had implanted exactly the way they should have. He held Bethany Michelle, while Kady cradled Nathaniel Eric. These were it for them. Their children. Their little family. They would raise and love them and cherish every moment they had with them. Just as they'd done with Grace.

Tucker hoped they both lived long happy lives. Someday they would talk to them about their older sister, show them pictures, and they would visit her grave together. She would always hold a special place in their hearts. She'd taught him that the important things in life might not last as long as one might like. Any of them could be taken in an instant. Life carried no guarantees.

It had taken him far too long to learn that message. He could have saved both Kady and himself a lot of heartache if he'd been able to understand this truth, that they needed to be grateful for the blessings of life and to take nothing for granted.

Carefully keeping Bethany against his chest, he leaned down and kissed Kady. "The nurse said your grandparents are here. They'll want to see the babies."

"They'll spoil them rotten." She sighed. "But I wouldn't have it any other way."

"I wouldn't either. Do you think your grandfather has finally forgiven me?" Tucker had been accepted back into the fold as if nothing had ever happened. As if he hadn't been a huge jerk for the last two years.

"He loves you. My whole family loves you. Probably more than they love me."

"Not true, but thank you. And I love *you*. Thanks for knocking some sense into me."

"You came to your senses all by yourself. I'm the one who had to be convinced in the end. No more secrets, okay?"

They'd caught the balloon back at the hospital, and Kady's original wedding rings were now back on her finger. Watching her thumb rub across those bands again and again was satisfying in a way that nothing else was.

"No more secrets." He'd been afraid that Kady's pregnancy might affect him physically, but it hadn't. They'd talked through his reservations, and she'd told him even if they never had sex again, she was okay. She loved him. Wanted to be with him.

They'd had sex, though. Lots of it.

He'd gone through genetic counseling with her, insisting even when she said it was no longer necessary. He'd done it anyway, the way he should have all those years ago. He never wanted her to feel that alone ever again.

He'd even asked if she wanted him to have his vasectomy reversed, saying for future babies they could use their own sperm and eggs and have the embryos tested before they were implanted. Kady said she was happy with the two babies they were going to have. They were enough.

Yes, they were.

And so was she.

He was back in Atlanta. Back in the house where they'd spent time with Grace. It had taken some careful planning as the New York hospital hadn't wanted to let him out of his contract, but in the end they'd capitulated when he'd worked out a compromise. He had to promise to come up for a month once a year when the new crop of medical students was doing its shadowing. Once the babies were old enough, Kady would join him.

Bethany squirmed against him and gave a thin cry. Tucker immediately tensed, only to find Kady's hand on his arm. "Hey, it's okay. She's okay."

He took a careful breath and blew it out. "You may have to talk me down from the ledge from time to time."

"We'll probably take turns standing on it. When that happens we'll just hold hands and get through it together."

"Together. That's one of my favorite words." He lowered himself into a chair beside the bed. "Why don't you try to get some sleep? I can either hold the babies or call the nurse to come and take them."

"You're actually willing to let them out of your sight?"

"What? No. I'd go down with them and wait until you're awake again."

Kady couldn't contain her laugh. "I want them to stay up here. There'll be plenty of time to sleep later." She tilted her head so it leaned against his arm. "Besides, I'm afraid I'll wake up and find this is all a dream."

"It is a dream. But it's very, very real. I'll be here when you wake up. So will Bethany and Nathaniel." He grinned. "Well, the babies and I might be in the nursery, depending on how strict they are about time schedules." The hospital did offer rooming in, but since Kady had needed a C-section they might be a little less accommodating to their request, even though Kady worked in this very unit. Doctors supposedly made the worst patients. Who knew?

"You look good holding her," Kady said. "I never believed this was possible."

"You look good holding him."

Settling a little deeper in the recliner, he did his best to soak in this moment, to imprint it on his memory—where he could retrieve it when times got tough.

One thing he knew for sure—he would never walk away from this woman ever again. Or his children.

He was right where he belonged. And this was where he would stay. For as long as they both should live.

* * * * *

LET'S TALK

Romance

For exclusive extracts, competitions and special offers, find us online:

f facebook.com/millsandboon

🄾 @millsandboonuk

🐦 @millsandboon

Or get in touch on 0844 844 1351*

For all the latest titles coming soon, visit millsandboon.co.uk/nextmonth

Want even more
ROMANCE?

Join our bookclub today!

'Mills & Boon books, the perfect way to escape for an hour or so.'

Miss W. Dyer

'Excellent service, promptly delivered and very good subscription choices.'

Miss A. Pearson

'You get fantastic special offers and the chance to get books before they hit the shops'

Mrs V. Hall

Visit millsandbook.co.uk/Bookclub and save on brand new books.

MILLS & BOON